Tales of Meadley
Stories 1-3

Liz Hedgecock

WHITE RHINO BOOKS

Copyright © Liz Hedgecock, 2023, 2024
(text and cover image)

All rights reserved. Apart from any use permitted under UK copyright law, no part of this publication may be reproduced, stored in a retrieval system, or transmitted, in any form or by any means, electronic, mechanical, photocopying, recording or otherwise, without the prior written permission of the copyright owner.

This is a work of fiction. Names, characters, businesses, places, events and incidents are either the products of the author's imagination or used in a fictitious manner. Any resemblance to actual persons, living or dead, or actual events is purely coincidental.

ISBN-13: 979-8303520585

To the volunteers: the people who step up and get things done

GNU Terry Pratchett

To the crafters, who knit, crochet and make the world brighter, one stitch at a time

To the independent shopkeepers, who serve our communities

Contents

The Book Swap	1
The Postbox Topper	73
The Corner Shop	157
The Secret Santa	241

The Book Swap

1

'*Becca.*'

Jolted out of her thoughts, Becca jerked upright. Everyone in the room was looking at her.

'Sorry,' she said, 'I was miles away.'

'We saw,' said the chair of the Parent-Teacher Association, a gilet-wearing, tousle-haired, immaculately manicured woman called Saffron. 'Would you like a recap?'

'Please,' said Becca. There was a huff from halfway down the meeting-room table where Mrs Hanratty, the teacher member of the PTA, was sitting.

'So,' said Saffron, 'we were just discussing the book swap.'

'The book swap?' Becca already regretted her decision to join the PTA. *It'll be a way to meet people and make friends*, she had thought, after a week of standing on her own in the playground at drop-off and pick-up, watching the other parents chat and giggle. *A good way to get back into doing things again. Low pressure.*

When the letter about admission to primary school had arrived, Becca realised with a shock that the decision would affect not just the next seven years of Ellie's life, but hers too. *Can I stand another seven years of this?* she thought, as she stirred a mug of packet soup after she had finally got Ellie to sleep. *No money, no social life, nothing but Ellie. And the local schools aren't up to much.* So she had done some research, moved to a small flat in leafy Meadley, and got Ellie into the excellent primary school.

And now here she was, facing the members of the PTA. With everyone around a large table, the meeting reminded her of *The Apprentice*, except the participants seemed far more capable and fearsome. So far, items on the agenda had included pulling strings to replace the school iPads with the latest versions, bidding for funding for solar panels, and organising an exchange visit to Nice so that year six could practise their French. Becca, who had expected a bake sale or maybe a school disco, slid down in her seat as figures flew about the room, along with words like logistics, leverage, and interoperability. Was that even a word?

'Yes, Becca, the book swap,' said Saffron, with a hint of weariness. 'Frankly, I'm as unimpressed as you sound, but in the absence of anyone else, here we are.'

'I'm afraid I don't—'

'You're new to Meadley, aren't you?' said Heather. If Saffron was Level Five scary, Heather was a three. Her gilet was fluffier, her nails less pointed, and Becca had actually seen her smile. 'The book swap is a former phone box on Beech Lane, not far from the school.'

'Oh,' said Becca. 'I come the other way.'

'I daresay you do,' said Heather. 'Now, the book swap is nothing to do with the school, but the thing is that old Mrs Val, who usually looks after it, is having a hip replaced and will be out of action for some time. As the school is nearby, the parish council asked us to take ownership of the book swap for a while. Literacy, and all that.' She waved a dismissive hand.

'I still don't see why the older children couldn't take it on,' said Saffron.

'SATs prep,' snapped Mrs Hanratty. 'Plus health and safety. You don't know where those books have been. With some of them, you wouldn't want to.'

'There's nothing to it,' said Heather. 'Checking it maybe once a week, removing any books which aren't fit to be there, tidying the shelves…' She eyed Becca speculatively. 'You said when you introduced yourself that you're not working right now.'

'I will be looking for a job once Ellie has settled

in,' said Becca. 'So I definitely couldn't commit to anything long-term.'

'Oh, it wouldn't be long-term,' said Heather. 'Just until Mrs Val is back on her feet. I'm sure she'll be raring to go before we know it. A contact from the council told me the Best Kept Middle-Sized Village inspectors will be paying Meadley a visit fairly soon, so we really must look our best.' She smiled at Becca, who was suddenly very aware of her faded jeans and the frayed hem of her top. She glanced at her nails and winced. She'd fallen into the habit of chewing them again.

'If someone else wants to do it, I won't stand in their way,' said Becca, in a last-ditch attempt to swerve her duty.

'It's not that I don't want to do it,' said Heather, 'but I'm already leading on the green energy bid. And we just opened a new office in Luxembourg, so I'm a bit stretched right now.'

'I'm extending my coaching practice,' said Saffron. 'When I finish here, I've got an in-depth business transformation session to deliver on Zoom.'

'I've got marking,' growled Mrs Hanratty.

'And as you haven't taken on any other responsibilities…' Heather let the words hang in the air like a bad smell.

Becca raised her hands in surrender. 'All right. I'll take a look at it tomorrow, after school drop-off, and think about it.'

'That's settled, then,' said Saffron. 'Alicia, minute that. Action for Becca. I'll follow up.'

Becca shivered involuntarily.

'Any other business? No? Good.' Saffron stood up and began packing things into her designer bucket bag. 'Heather, can you let me have five minutes? Rosie, I need to touch base with you: playground tomorrow? Mrs Hanratty, we must have a word about accreditation, but we can do that some other time. Thanks, everyone. Oh yes, and the headteacher has assured me he *will* attend the next PTA meeting.' She beckoned Heather over.

Becca took her coat off the back of her chair and put it on. She had expected people to linger for a chat, but they were all striding to the door. *Probably going home to family dinner. Maybe their partners are cooking.* She buttoned her coat and went into the corridor.

Ellie was colouring in a picture, her tongue poking out with concentration and one of her mousy plaits working its way free of its bobble. 'Here's your mummy!' said the teaching assistant brightly. 'She's been good as gold,' she added, standing up, gathering the coloured pencils and dropping them in the pot. 'Come on, Ellie, time to go home.'

Becca helped her daughter on with her coat and located the mitten which, as always, was halfway up her left sleeve. 'What's for dinner, Mummy?'

'Spaghetti bolognese,' said Becca.

'Ooh, yummy,' said the teaching assistant.

'Hopefully,' said Becca, though she didn't hold out much hope for the jar of sauce and the own-brand pasta sitting on the kitchen counter. She took Ellie's hand and followed everyone else into the playground.

'You took *ages*, Mummy,' said Ellie, pulling on her hand. 'What were you doing?'

Becca considered how to answer. Making friends . . . no. 'Helping with school stuff,' she said, eventually.

'Ooh. Like what?' Their footsteps sounded unnaturally loud in the darkness. Becca hurried Ellie along until they were on the well-lit street.

'Um, I'm really not sure.'

2

Becca kissed Ellie on the cheek. 'Go on, trouble, you'd better get in line. The bell will ring any minute.' *And if you're in the line, maybe one of the other kids will talk to you.* She was worried that after two weeks at school, Ellie would chatter happily to her about Mrs Shaw, her class teacher, and Mrs Daniels, the teaching assistant, but hardly ever mentioned a classmate. *Make friends, Ellie. Don't be like me.*

'Mrs Shaw won't come out for ages,' said Ellie, bottom lip protruding, blue eyes round and sad. 'We're always last.'

'You should still be in line, ready for her.' Becca eyed the old-fashioned bell on the wall, waiting for someone to tug it into noisy life.

'OK, Mummy,' said Ellie, and skipped off to the line. Just as she joined it, the bell rang. Ellie looked round and waved at her. 'Bye, Mummy!'

'Bye, Ellie, have a good day!' Becca called. She edged backwards to the wire fence. She couldn't leave, not until Ellie was safely in school, but she could prepare for a quick getaway.

Or she could have done if it wasn't for Mrs Shaw. The lines of bigger children – not much bigger, but still –progressed jerkily into the school, with occasional deserters running back for a forgotten lunchbox or dropped mitten, but the reception class fidgeted on the playground like new recruits waiting for the arrival of the sergeant major.

Just when Becca thought they would be there all day, the reception class door opened and Mrs Shaw walked outside. 'Good morning, everyone!'

'Good morning, Mrs Shaw,' the line chorused raggedly.

'We've got lots to do today, so let's come inside quickly and quietly.'

Cheek, thought Becca. *You're the one who's kept us standing here.*

The children filed in immediately, only occasionally knocking into the child in front, dropping something, or turning to wave to their parents yet again. Finally the last child made their way through the door, which was abruptly pulled shut.

Becca let out a relieved breath and scuttled to the gate, but the other parents had beaten her to it. There was already a queue to leave, complicated further by two women, both towing wailing children, trying to get into the playground. Becca leaned against the fence and waited. *At least that's not me*, she thought. *Just imagine.* Today was the latest she had dared to leave it, arriving in the playground five minutes before the bell was due to ring. She was pretty sure Saffron and Heather would be in the junior playground, if they weren't cutting deals over croissants and coffee, but best not to take any chances.

The queue was dwindling now, and she joined it. Ten minutes at a fast walk and she would be at the flat, putting the kettle on and searching a job site or two. Maybe.

'*There* you are.'

Becca's heart sank. Saffron, of course, resplendent in her furry gilet and a matching fur hat which looked as if it ought to belong to the Queen of Narnia. *Don't accept any Turkish Delight.* While Saffron was smiling, her tone conveyed that Becca ought to have been quicker about getting to a place where she could be apprehended.

'Hi, Saffron,' Becca ventured.

'I'm sure you're on your way to the book swap,' said Saffron. 'Unless you've already visited?'

'Well, I—'

'What am I saying? Of course you haven't. I checked it when I was bringing my two in and it's still a disgrace. But now that you've taken it on…'

'Yes,' said Becca, faintly.

'I knew we could count on you,' said Saffron, patting her on the shoulder. 'I've just been chatting with Declan – the headteacher, you know – and I assured him you would restore the book swap to its former glory.'

'Thank you so much,' said Becca.

'My pleasure,' said Saffron, and gave her a smile more suited for a child who had managed to put the round shape in the round hole of the shape-sorter. 'Oh Rosie, do you have that five minutes you promised me?' And she was off, her knee-high leather boots squeaking as she hastened to apprehend another hapless parent.

Becca sighed. *Stitched up like a holey sock.* She ambled to the gate – presumably even Saffron wouldn't tell her to hurry – and followed the wire fence in the opposite direction to the way she would normally go. Towards the book swap.

***

The closer Becca got to the red phone box on Beech Lane, the more fervently she hoped for a miracle. Not that she was religious, but if some divine being had pulled a blinder out of their box of tricks…

However, it was not to be. With every step the windows of the book swap grew grimier and the books within more untidy. In the front window was a sheet of lined paper with *BOOK SWAP* written on it in wavering capitals. At least, that was what Becca presumed it said. One side had come unstuck and the sign had swivelled round, so in reality it said *OK AP*.

Maybe it'll be better when I open the door. Maybe the books themselves are fine. Maybe it just needs Blu-Tack, a damp cloth and a bit of a tidy. She gripped the tarnished silver handle and pulled. Then she let go and stepped back, her nose wrinkling of its own accord. 'Oof.'

What was that smell? Becca sucked in a lungful of fresh air and considered. It combined the mustiness of old books with bottom notes of wet dog and perhaps an accent of urine. She moved cautiously forward and peered through the glass. The books sat higgledy-piggledy on the shelves, in some places two deep, while elsewhere there were gaps like missing teeth. Horror novels loomed over mysteries, while steamy-looking romances snuggled up to children's books.

Becca felt in her pocket and found a clean tissue to cover her nose and mouth. She steeled herself, then advanced and wrenched the door open again.

The smell persisted even through the handkerchief. Becca glanced at the floor, half expecting to see a puddle, but presumably it had dried. *What if there are mice? Or rats?* She let go of the door and walked away, hearing it creak then clunk shut. *Like a coffin lid in a horror film, or the front door of a haunted house.*

She wiped her fingers on the tissue and wished she still carried hand sanitiser. *There's no way I'm dealing with that*, she thought, her mouth setting in a firm line as she marched down the street. *If Saffron wants it doing so badly, she can do it herself. I'll tell her I'm jobhunting – no, I am jobhunting. I'll start as soon as I get home. Anything to make sure I never have to open that door and smell that smell ever again.*

3

Becca hurried through the drizzle to school. It had been a trying day. She had, as she had promised herself, begun looking for jobs. This had involved searching the website of the local newspaper on her phone, then the various job boards. 'If I had a car...' she muttered. 'Or I didn't have to work within school hours, or the buses weren't rubbish.'

She pinched the bridge of her nose and scrolled through the list yet again. There was one – School Administrator, part-time, not Ellie's school, but one a short bus ride away. But... She eyed the list of duties. *It's been so long...*

She had always intended to go back to work after maternity leave, but Phil had convinced her it was a bad idea. 'Childcare costs are ridiculous,' he had said. 'You'd end up paying to go to work. It would actually save money if you stayed at home. You could take

Ellie to playgroups and things.'

'I suppose... But I like my job and the team are great. I don't want to give up work.'

'It wouldn't be for ever. Just while Ellie's little, until she goes to school... Maybe when the preschool grant kicks in you could find something part-time. Or get an Avon round, if you can't find a proper job. You could wheel Ellie round with you.'

She was lying on the sofa, exhausted, with Ellie fast asleep in the crook of her elbow, having dropped off in the middle of a feed. 'Becca,' Phil said, and she turned her head on the cushion, too tired and too apprehensive about waking Ellie to move any further. 'Face facts. I work away a lot. How will you cope with holding down a job and looking after a baby?'

And that was that. Becca had stayed at home, working through never-ending piles of washing and ironing, cooking meals to tempt Ellie, who was a fussy eater, then making dinner for when Phil got in, usually late. In return, just before Ellie's third birthday, Phil met Ariane on one of his work trips. She was twenty-four, dynamic, didn't have milk stains on her top, and kept up with current affairs. 'She takes care of herself,' he had said, in explanation. 'Works out, gets her nails done, that sort of thing.'

'I'd work out and get my nails done if I had any spare time or money,' said Becca.

'No you wouldn't,' said Phil. 'When you put Ellie

down for the night you stare at the TV like a zombie.'

Becca opened her mouth to defend herself, then closed it. Things dragged on uneasily for a few more months, mostly because Becca was too overwhelmed by the idea of starting again with nothing in the bank. Phil had weaselled his way out of marrying her when she became pregnant. *Always an excuse*, she thought, as she wiped the dining table following another messy meal. *Let's have a proper wedding once the baby's born, Becca... We can't afford a wedding and a baby, Becca... There doesn't seem much point now, Becca... What a fool I was.*

Eventually, though, after several heavy hints, Phil had offered her money to help with the rent until she found her feet, and Becca had moved into a small flat half a mile away. Her parents had urged her to move back home with them in Scotland – they had never taken to Phil – but pride kept Becca from complying. She had thought staying near what she knew would help, but gradually people drifted away. Or perhaps she'd pushed them away. She wasn't sure which.

She looked at the advert again. 'Who would employ me?' she asked herself. 'They probably wouldn't even give me an interview.' She swiped out of her browser, put the phone face down, and went to make herself a cup of tea. A hot drink would warm her up, and there would be no need to put the heating on.

She had kept herself busy by giving the flat a good clean, then going to the cheapest food shop in the village to pick up some bits and pieces. There was a cheaper supermarket in town, but that would involve taking a bus, an expensive bus, and carrying it all home. Something was bound to go wrong. She had checked the shop windows and the village noticeboard for job opportunities, too, but there had been nothing.

As she trudged along the road which led to the school, wrapped up in a big coat, scarf, gloves and woolly hat, Becca remembered Froggy, her little green runabout, who had run like a dream until the day he wouldn't start and was pronounced not worth fixing.

'We don't really need two cars,' Phil had said. 'Everything you need is a short walk away. We could go down to one car and save money. And it's good for the environment. We'd still have mine for the big shop.'

'Good for the environment,' she muttered, as the cold wind found its way between the loops of her scarf and stung her neck. Cars glided past, parking as close as they could to the school, and parents got out, exclaiming at the weather.

As usual on wet days, it took even longer for the classroom doors to open. Becca waited, shifting from foot to foot, hands rammed in her pockets, but by a small miracle, the reception-class door opened first. Mrs Daniels stood there, looking for the parent to match each child. Becca craned her neck, but she didn't see Ellie.

Child after child was reunited with their parent, but still Becca waited. At last, when the strands of hair that had escaped from her hat were thoroughly damp, Ellie appeared. Becca waved and Ellie made to go to her, but Mrs Daniels held her back, scanning the playground in every direction but Becca's.

She stepped forward. 'I'm here.'

'Oh yes, so you are,' said Mrs Daniels. 'Silly me. I didn't recognise you, all wrapped up.'

'It's raining,' said Becca.

'Yes, well. See you tomorrow, Ellie. Don't forget to tell your mummy what you've got in your bag.' She released Ellie, who ran to Becca and took her hand.

'What have you got in your bag?' Becca asked, as Ellie towed her to the gate. 'Let me put your hood up.'

'Books!'

'A new reading book? We haven't finished the last one.'

'No, for the book swap! A big girl brought them. I have to give them to you. Because you run the book swap.' Something in Becca's face changed Ellie's excitement into confusion. 'That's right, isn't it, Mummy? Mrs Shaw said you did. And she said I was a sort of book monitor.' Ellie puffed her chest out.

'She said I should have a badge.'

'Did she,' said Becca.

'Can we go now?'

Becca opened her mouth to say that it was raining and they'd do it tomorrow, then changed her mind. *If Ellie sees it, dirty, smelly and damp, she'll understand why I don't want to look after it.* 'Yes,' she said, and they turned away from home.

Becca's footsteps slowed as they approached the phone box, even grimmer through a filter of rain, but Ellie pulled her towards it. 'Come on, Mummy! Let's put the books in.'

Becca opened the door. 'Just put them on the shelf, Ellie, anywhere will do.'

Ellie slotted the books carefully into one of the gaps. There were three: a phonics book, a picture book about The Elves and the Shoemaker, and something called *Beast Quest*. 'There,' she said, with satisfaction. 'I'll tell Mrs Shaw, then everyone will know. Maybe they'll bring books too.'

'Maybe,' said Becca. 'Let's head home before this gets worse.'

Ellie skipped by her side, her mittened hand in Becca's. 'We went to the book swap!' she sang. 'We went to the book swap!'

Becca looked down at her. 'Did you like it?'

'Yes,' said Ellie. 'But it's sad.'

'It's dirty,' said Becca. 'The books aren't in any

order. And it smells.'

'That's why it's sad,' said Ellie. 'We can make it feel better, can't we?' She gazed up at Becca. 'Can't we?'

There was no way out. 'Yes.'

'Hooray!' Ellie did an extra big skip. 'I'll make a new sign at home. We can tidy it after school tomorrow.'

'Maybe,' said Becca. She pulled out her phone and checked the weather forecast for the next day. Sunny. But Ellie wasn't setting foot in that phone box until it was less disgusting, which meant she would be cleaning it while Ellie was in school tomorrow.

'I'll use my best felt tips,' said Ellie. 'The ones Daddy gave me. And I'll put the sign in my bag to show Mrs Shaw tomorrow.'

'Yes, why not,' said Becca. And as she wondered what she had got herself into, a gust of rain hit her in the face.

4

'Are you going to the book swap today, Mummy?'

'Yes, Ellie, to clean it. Now please will you put your shoes on? We'll be late if you don't hurry.'

'I'm excited.' Ellie sat on the little stool by the front door of the flat, her toes in one shoe, gazing up at Becca. 'Can we go after school? So I can put my sign up?'

'Yes, but only if you get your shoes and coat on in the next two minutes.'

Ellie rammed her feet into her shoes, then stood on tiptoe to unhook her coat. She couldn't quite manage it and Becca unhooked it for her, laughing. 'Maybe the book swap isn't such a bad thing if it gets you to stop daydreaming!'

'Is daydreaming bad?' asked Ellie. She put her left arm in the sleeve and tried to pull the coat round herself.

'No,' said Becca, 'not at all. Just inconvenient sometimes, when people are in a hurry.'

'Is the book swap bad?'

Becca sighed. 'No, just messy.' She secured Ellie's flailing right arm and guided it into her coat sleeve.

'I nearly did it, Mummy,' said Ellie.

'I know. We'd better get moving.'

Ellie didn't move. 'You forgot something.'

Becca patted her pockets. Purse, phone, keys waiting on the hook. 'I don't think so.'

'Cleaning stuff? For the book swap?'

'I'm going to the book swap later, Ellie. I'm not lugging a load of cleaning products to school with me. Now do come *on*.' Her tone was sharper than she had intended, and Ellie's lip quivered.

'Are you cross? I'm sorry, Mummy.'

'It's OK.' Becca gave her daughter a gentle hug, then got her keys. 'Come on, time to go.'

They arrived in the playground as the reception-class line was filing in. Becca kissed Ellie on the top of her head and half ran with her to the line. Of course, Mrs Shaw was at the head of it. 'Good morning, Ellie,' she said. 'Did you get held up?'

'We were having a discussion,' said Becca.

'Ahh,' said Mrs Shaw, and looked very wise. 'I'm sure we'll see you bright and **early this afternoon.**'

Becca thought about saluting, but decided the potential consequences for Ellie weren't worth it.

'Sure,' she said, and watched Ellie file into the classroom.

Back at the flat, she checked the cupboard under the sink for materials. There was a half-pack of J-cloths, rubber gloves, some all-purpose cleaner, and a duster with holes in it. *I don't mind throwing that away.* She found a tote bag, and as an afterthought put in a can of Febreze she had bought when Phil dropped his kebab in their sitting room after a late-night session. The smell had lingered for weeks. Finally, she boiled the kettle, quarter-filled a bucket with hot soapy water, then stuck a mop in it. *This is probably overkill*, she thought, eyeing the small pile sitting by her front door.

The book swap looked marginally less dingy today. Becca assumed that was the effect of the sunshine rather than any actual improvement. She set down her bucket gratefully, pulled on the gloves, and opened the door.

'Oh, for heaven's sake.' A carrier bag sat on the floor, books spilling out. She picked up a couple. One had no cover, and a couple of loose pages fluttered to the ground like dead leaves. Becca bit back a swearword, seized the bag and dumped it on the pavement. She reached for the Febreze and sprayed it liberally in the air. Finally, she put on a fabric mask she had found stuffed in a drawer and set to work.

The floor of the book swap responded surprisingly

well to being mopped. After a couple of goes, the dirt began to lift. Becca smiled as she pushed her mop into the corners. 'That's better, isn't it?'

You're talking to a phone box.

Becca's face grew warm. Perhaps that was the exercise, though. *So what?* she thought. *No one's around to hear me.* She inspected the water in the bucket, which looked as if an alligator might raise its head any minute. 'That'll do,' she said, and put the bucket outside. 'Now for the windows.' She took down the *OK AP* notice and rummaged in her bag of supplies.

But no matter how much all-purpose cleaner she squirted on the glass, most of the grime refused to shift. Becca wondered whether the windows were tinted until a small clear patch appeared and made the rest of the glass seem even dirtier. *It's ridiculous*, she thought, throwing down her cloth in disgust. *At this rate I'll need a whole bottle of this stuff for one bit of glass.* Then she glanced at the shelves. Her eyes gleamed above her mask and she reached for a duster.

A few minutes later the duster was scored with dark lines, but the shelves were noticeably cleaner. Becca took off her mask and inhaled slowly. The book swap was still a bit musty, but not actively unpleasant. Her eyes watered, but that was probably disturbed dust. *Historic dust. And that's mostly gone.* She inspected the duster. *Hot water will fix that.*

'Right, that's enough for now,' she said. 'I'll come back when I know what to do about the windows.'

She reversed out of the phone box, turned and—

'Oof!' She collided with a white open-necked shirt.

'Oh, sorry,' said the man wearing it. He was in his late thirties, maybe early forties, pleasant-looking, with dark hair greying at the sides. He was also wearing a smart navy suit, which made the orange plastic bag he was holding seem incongruous. 'I was just—' He held up the bag.

Becca's eyes narrowed. 'Are you dumping those?'

'Not dumping, exactly.'

Becca held out a hand for the bag, and on receipt, peered in. Children's books, well past their best days. She extracted one at random and stared at its ripped cover. 'Do you think this is fit to go into the book swap? Really?'

'OK, maybe not that one, but I'm in a bit of a rush, so—'

'So you're dumping them here for me to deal with,' Becca snapped. 'Thanks a bunch.'

He sighed. 'Look, I'm on my way back from a meeting. The charity bookshop was closed.'

'Whatever. Off you go. You carry on being busy and important, and I'll deal with this.'

He stepped back, raising his hands in surrender, and Becca was gratified to see a mark on his shirt.

'Won't happen again, if that makes you feel better.'

'It's a start,' said Becca, and watched him walk to his car. He got in and buckled up, and it glided away without a sound. *Electric. That figures.* She turned to the book swap. 'If any of those books are worth keeping, I'll let Ellie put them in later.' She emptied her bucket into a nearby drain, packed up, and set off home.

As she walked, she found herself speculating about the book dumper. *Unusual to see a man in a suit dropping off children's books. Wonder what he does? Maybe he's a single parent like me.*

Or maybe his wife knew he was passing the charity bookshop and handed them to him when he was leaving this morning. 'Can you do something with these? The kids have grown out of them, and it's only five minutes out of your way.' Becca wrinkled her nose, then stopped at the front door of the flats, put the bucket down and fished in her pocket for keys.

Once home, Becca put everything away and washed her hands. She studied herself in the bathroom mirror: hair scragged back in a ponytail, her face framed by a couple of sweaty strands. She had a smudge of dirt on her forehead, and the mask had left faint red lines across her nose and cheeks. She giggled. *I'm not surprised you scared him off!*

She treated herself to a quick shower, then settled on the sofa to go through the bags of books.

Occasionally the book dumper came to mind, but when he did, she shoved him out again and carried on.

5

'I was hoping I'd catch you.'

Becca turned, guilt sending a shiver down her spine, though she wasn't sure what to be guilty about. There was bound to be something.

Standing beside her was a woman who seemed vaguely familiar. 'Rosie,' she said. 'We met at the PTA.'

'Oh. Yes. Sorry, I—'

'I wanted to say that you're doing a great job with the book swap. I passed it on my way here and it's looking much better. Those windows were a disgrace before. And it doesn't smell!'

Becca felt her face flush for what seemed to be the tenth time that day. 'Oh, it wasn't anything, just Febreze and vinegar and a good scrub.' *The cheapest vinegar I could find*, she added, to herself. She had been amazed at how it cut through the greyish-brown film that coated the glass. *If it doesn't still smell like a chip shop, Ellie can put up her sign.*

'I'll get Eva and George to go through their bookshelves and pass on anything they've outgrown,' Rosie said. 'I wouldn't have put them in the swap before, because it was so smelly and dirty that it would have ruined them.'

'I suppose,' said Becca. *It's a vicious circle*, she thought. *People put their tatty unloved books there, so no one goes, the book swap gets worse, and the books get worse.* 'Thank you,' she said. 'I'll check the shelves and remove anything that shouldn't be there.'

'That's a good idea,' said Rosie. 'Do you need any help? I mean, we're all busy, but—'

'No, it's fine,' said Becca. 'I can manage.'

'Mummy!'

It was Ellie's voice. She was at the reception-class door, practically jumping up and down with frustration.

'Sorry,' she said. She held out her hand and Ellie ran to her.

'I thought you'd never look, Mummy,' she scolded. 'Can we go to the book swap now?'

Becca rolled her eyes, mostly for Rosie's benefit. 'I feel as if I've spent all day in the book swap. But yes.'

'Let me know when there's room for more books,' said Rosie, and drifted towards the door for year two.

'I've got more books,' said Ellie. 'And the sign.

Mrs Shaw said it was lovely. She put a marble in the jar. That's my first marble.'

'What does that mean?'

Ellie gave a little sigh. 'When the jar's full, we get a class treat.' She gazed up at Becca. 'Didn't you have marbles at school?'

***

Ellie skipped as they neared the book swap. 'It's clean!'

'It's certainly cleaner,' said Becca. 'Hopefully it'll stay that way.' The leaves on the tree by the phone box had begun to turn. The afternoon light caught them, transforming each into a bright gold coin.

'Mrs Shaw gave me this for the sign.' Ellie rummaged in her school bag and produced a folded blue paper towel, in which was a ball of Blu-Tack.

'Oh good,' said Becca. 'I didn't think of that.'

'Mrs Shaw did,' said Ellie, with an air that suggested Mrs Shaw was a superior human being.

'Good for her. Let's put your sign up. Ooh, wait – let's take a picture of you with it first.'

Ellie stood in front of the book swap, held the sign up and beamed. One of her socks was falling down. Regardless, Becca snapped a picture on her phone. Then she divided the Blu-Tack into four, pressed a piece into each corner of the sign and opened the door of the book swap.

'Careful, Mummy! Don't break the glass.'

'Don't worry.' Becca made sure the sign was straight and pushed it into place.

'Can I look?'

'Yes, but don't go in the road.'

Ellie ran a few steps, then turned. Joy spread over her face. 'Everyone will know it's a book swap now!' She ran back, pulled four books from her bag and handed them to Becca, one by one.

When she came to the last book, she didn't let go. 'Mummy…'

'Yes, Ellie?'

'Could we borrow this? It looks fun.'

Becca glanced at the cover. *The Magic Key*, it said.

'I like Biff and Chip,' said Ellie, 'but I haven't read this one yet. I'm on Pink band. This is Blue band.'

'Then we'll borrow it,' said Becca. 'We can put it in the book swap when we finish it, or maybe you could put in a book you don't read any more.'

Not that Ellie had many books. Phil had objected to book-buying on the grounds that there was a perfectly good library nearby and she would only grow out of them. But the perfectly good library was where they had lived before. Phil gave her an allowance for Ellie, which he said was more than he was obliged to do. However, once the bills were paid and food bought, plus school uniform and essentials, little was left for luxuries such as books. Books were Christmas and birthday presents or occasional surprises from Gran and Grandad, not a way of life.

Ellie put the book in her bag. 'Can we read it tonight? I won't know all the words, but I'll try.'

'I know you will, sweetheart,' said Becca, and hugged her.

***

The next day, once she had dropped Ellie at school, Becca nipped home to collect the things she had left ready. She returned to the book swap with several bags for life, cleaning materials, and a set of collapsible steps. It was sunny again, and she had to admit the phone box was looking much brighter, not just because of the pink and blue flowers on Ellie's sign.

'Right,' she said. 'A bit of outside work, then sorting the books.' She placed the steps, climbed up, and wiped the dirt from the front *TELEPHONE* sign. 'That's better: people can see you properly now.' She leaned back to admire her handiwork and nearly overbalanced at a loud honk behind her.

Becca grabbed the top of the steps to steady herself, glared at the passing car, then giggled. *Someone said hello.* She turned to the book swap, gave it a little pat, and climbed down. She moved round the box until all four signs were clean.

She opened the door and gazed at the shelves, then began checking through them. Once you'd taken out the really shabby books – and there weren't many –

the rest was fine. It just needed organising.

She grouped books in categories: thrillers, mysteries, non-fiction, romance, and children's books on the bottom shelves where they could be reached. As she searched through the shelves, she frowned. *Those weren't there before.* Three books that belonged together. She pulled one out. *His Dark Materials: Northern Lights*, she read. It wasn't new – it had definitely been read – but it was in good condition.

Someone must have dropped them off, she thought, and felt a little glow inside. For the first time in longer than she could remember, she was proud of herself. 'See, people are bringing you nice things,' she said to the book swap. She smiled, and carried on sorting the books.

6

Gradually, word spread. Ellie's school bag contained a book or two for the swap every day, often with a little note saying thank you. When the book or two became five, six or seven, Becca asked Mrs Shaw whether it would be possible to have a book-swap box somewhere in school that she could collect from.

'What a good idea,' said Mrs Shaw. 'That might be a library project.'

A week later, she summoned Becca in the playground. 'The library helpers have found and decorated a box and it will live in reception,' she said. 'If you're calling into the office, you can take a look.'

'Thanks,' said Becca. She could feel her cheeks and her neck going pink.

Once Ellie had gone into the classroom, Becca went round to the main entrance and rang for admission, rather overawed. She half-expected to be told off but someone buzzed her in. And in the foyer was a large cardboard box, covered in red and blue stripy paper and decorated with stuck-on multicoloured letters: *BOOK SWAP BOX*. There was already a small pile of books inside.

'Are you the book-swap lady?' asked the receptionist. Her badge said *Angie*. 'I've got a sign for you.' She reached below the counter and produced a large piece of card. On a cream background was a collage: two rows of bunting. Each flag had a letter on it, spelling out *TAKE A BOOK, LEAVE A BOOK*.

'Oh!' said Becca. 'It's lovely. Who made it?'

'The library helpers,' said Angie. 'They're very active.'

'Wow. Can you say thank you to them for me?'

'I'll let the English lead know. Will you take the books, too?'

'Oh yes, I should, shouldn't I?' Becca bent over the box to hide her embarrassment. 'Shall I call in once a week?'

'That seems sensible.'

Becca made a hasty exit, sign and books tucked under her arm.

The sign would just fit above the top shelf of the book swap. Becca wondered if one of the enterprising library helpers had visited and measured up. She tried to remember what she had done in the last years of primary school. Nothing so useful, certainly.

She slipped the books from school into a convenient gap among the children's books and stepped back, sign in hand.

'What are you doing?'

Becca jumped. Standing nearby was a middle-aged woman in jeans and a puffer jacket. Her hair was in a tight ponytail, erupting in a mass of blonde curls at the top of her head.

'I was just— I take care of the book swap. I need to fetch some steps to put this sign up.' She displayed the sign and smiled, but her smile faded beneath the woman's unblinking gaze. 'Um, do you like books? It's free. You can take one if you want.'

'I'd like the time to read,' the woman said, stony-faced. 'I'd like the time to mess around playing house with a phone box.'

'I'm sorry, I—'

'I do the early clean at the school, you see, and now I'm off to my next job.'

'I am looking for a job,' said Becca, humbly.

'Are you really,' said the woman, and snorted.

'Well, not at this exact moment, but I've just dropped my daughter at school.'

'You don't have to make excuses to me,' said the woman. 'You carry on with your book box.'

'Um, thanks,' said Becca, but the woman was already walking away. Her trainers squeaked on the pavement.

Becca walked home, watching out for the woman, skirting any bus shelter where she might be waiting. She carried the sign facing inwards, suddenly ashamed to be seen with it. *I shouldn't be doing this. I should be applying for jobs or starting a business. I should be doing something to improve Ellie's life. And mine. Learning skills, if nothing else. Not messing about with this.*

But they asked me to do it.

And you always do as you're told, don't you?

She winced, and quickened her pace.

Her phone buzzed as she pulled out her keys. *I'll look when I get in*, she thought, manoeuvring the sign carefully through the doorway.

When she checked her phone, she was glad that she had waited.

Hey Bex, I can't take Ellie this weekend. Something's come up. Next weekend should be fine though. I'll send you a bit of money to buy her a treat, so she knows I'm thinking of her. Make sure you say it's from me. Phil

Becca sighed, imagining Ellie's disappointed face. She still believed in her father and Becca did her best not to interfere with that, even when Phil was at his most annoying. Even when he called her Bex, which she hated. She flicked the kettle on and hit *Reply*.

Thanks for letting me know. Make sure you do take Ellie next weekend, she loves spending time with you.

Becca

To be entirely honest, she wasn't sure that Ellie did love spending time with her father. When asked, Ellie always said she had had a nice time and showed Becca a trinket or a new hair bobble, but she never seemed enthusiastic. Phil ought to spend time with her, though, as her parent. Weekends had been agreed, and even if he managed two-thirds of them, maybe less, it was better than nothing.

Becca made herself a cup of tea and eyed the sign, propped up in the tiny hallway. *It can't stay here. Besides, the library helpers will expect to see it. And Ellie probably knows about it too.* She sighed, took a gulp of her tea, which was still far too hot, and went in search of something to put the sign up with.

***

Becca moved cautiously, burdened with steps, the sign, and a bag containing sticky tape, Blu-Tack and scissors. Then she realised the woman who had accosted her earlier would be at work by now, and relaxed.

'Back again,' she said as she reached the book swap, and looked around before patting it on one corner. She opened the door, balanced the sign on a shelf, and unfolded her steps.

As she had thought, the sign fitted snugly above the top of the shelves. It wouldn't need much to hold it. She found the Blu-Tack and pressed the sign in place. 'There.' She nodded at the sign and descended the steps.

As she did, something caught her eye. A book spine: *Wyrd Sisters – Terry Pratchett*. It was at her eye level. She had read a couple of Terry Pratchett books, but not this one. She reached for it, then paused. *It looks—* She took the book out to confirm it. *It looks new.* The spine was uncreased, the cover pristine. *Could it be the same person as before? The one who left the His Dark Materials books?*

She felt guilty for taking the book, as if she was stealing it. *I'll put it back when I've read it*, she reasoned. *It's meant to be borrowed. It's a book swap.* Nevertheless, she hid the book in her bag, and was glad to be on her way home.

She meant to read just a few pages, to see what the book was like. She only noticed the time when her stomach growled. *Oh dear.* She put a couple of slices of bread in the toaster. *I'll eat a quick lunch and check the job sites.* But somehow the book found its way into her hand again, and then she was too far through it to stop. *If I finish it, I can get on with what I should be doing.*

She read the last page, sighed a long, satisfied sigh and checked her phone. She had ten minutes until she needed to set off for school pickup. On impulse, she went to the chest of drawers. In the top drawer was a pad of letter paper and a few matching envelopes, possibly a relic of a school penpal long ago.

Becca found a pen and pondered what to say.

Thank you for leaving Wyrd Sisters at the book swap, she wrote. *It was very kind, especially as the book looks new. If you don't mind, I'll keep it for a little while to reread. I read it so quickly that I might have missed bits.*

Can I ask whether you also left the His Dark Materials books?

Thank you again,

Becca

PS I'm looking after the book swap temporarily.

She addressed the envelope – *To the person who left a copy of Wyrd Sisters here* – put the note in and stuck down the flap. Then she grabbed her coat, put the envelope in her pocket, and hurried to collect Ellie.

7

Two days later, at pick-up time, Ellie was at the classroom door when it opened. 'There's Mummy!' she cried, and Mrs Daniels let her go with a smile. 'Guess where we went today!' She barrelled into Becca, knocking the breath out of her, and wrapped her arms around her hips.

'I have no idea,' said Becca, laughing, when she got her breath back. 'Where did you go today?'

'We went to the book swap! It was a class trip for two of our school values.'

'Your which?' Ellie was quite muffled, and Becca wondered if she had heard right.

'Our *values*, Mummy. We had to put bright-yellow jackets on and walk in pairs. Olivia asked me to walk with her.'

'Oh good. Is Olivia your friend?'

'Of course she is, Mummy,' said Ellie, with a note

of exasperation in her voice. 'Anyway. Mrs Shaw was at the front and Mrs Daniels was at the back. We all took a book from the big box and put it in the book swap. Mrs Shaw says we have to visit with a grown-up and choose a book.' Ellie finally came up for air. 'Can we go now?'

'Could we make it next week?'

Ellie's jaw dropped. 'Mummy!'

Becca laughed. 'It was a joke. Come on, then.'

She said goodbye to Claire and Debs, two other reception-class mums she had started chatting to on the playground. Ellie gripped her hand, as if worried she might go the wrong way, and they set off.

If anything, Becca felt guilty. She hadn't returned to the book swap since leaving that note. Partly because she wasn't sure she wanted to know whether there was a reply, or even that it had been picked up, but also because she had spent too much time there recently. Instead she had cleaned the flat, tackling everything from light fittings to skirting boards. She had also overhauled her wardrobe, removing the tops and leggings faded and stretched out of shape through years of wear. She put them in a charity bag, and when she tied the handles together and left it by the gate she felt several pounds lighter.

'So what are the school values?' she asked.

'One is responsibility, for keeping the book swap tidy. Mrs Shaw says you have the main responsibility.

And when she said "Ellie's mummy" everyone looked at me!'

'Gosh,' said Becca. 'I suppose I do. What was the other value?'

'Community, because the book swap is part of our village and it's for everyone. There are three other values, too. Come on, Mummy, I'll race you!' Ellie ran to the phone box and pulled at the door, but couldn't open it. 'Mummyyy!' she wailed, then burst out laughing.

She isn't the same child, thought Becca as she hurried over. For a moment she felt a pang that Ellie didn't need to cling to her any more, then shook it off. *Once she would never have dreamt of running ahead and she'd have waited for me to open the door. Now she wants to do things herself.*

That's probably school, she thought, as she opened the door for Ellie, who immediately began searching for her book. *But this helps, too*. And she ran her hand along the bright-red paintwork.

'Here it is,' said Ellie, pulling out *The Highway Rat*. 'This is the book I put in.'

'Oh yes,' said Becca. 'That's nice.' She glanced at the shelves automatically to check their neatness, and froze.

Propped against the books on a higher shelf, well past a child's reach, was a white envelope with *Becca* written on it in neat black pen.

Becca took it down and stood looking at it.

'What is it, Mummy?' Ellie asked. 'Is it for you?'

'It has my name on it,' said Becca.

'Then it's for you. Aren't you going to open it?'

'Maybe later,' said Becca, and shoved it in her jeans pocket. 'Now, are you taking that book home, or do you want to choose another?'

Ellie spent ten minutes flicking through different books and putting them back neatly before deciding that yes, she would take *The Highway Rat*.

***

At the flat, Becca settled Ellie at the kitchen table with a colouring book while she made her toast.

'Mrs Shaw?' said Ellie.

Becca paused, butter knife in the air. 'I think you mean Mummy.'

'Sorry, Mummy,' said Ellie. 'Can I go to the toilet, please?'

'Of course you can,' said Becca. 'You don't have to ask.'

'We do at school,' said Ellie. She slid off her chair and ran out.

Becca chuckled, then fished the envelope from her pocket and ripped it open.

Dear Becca,

Thank you for your note, and I'm glad you enjoyed the book. Of course you can keep it to reread, if you like.

I wanted to thank you for looking after the book swap. It needed someone to take it in hand, and it is much better now.

Thank you for stepping up, from all of us.

Becca stared at the letter until she heard the toilet flush. Quickly, she stuffed the letter in the envelope and rammed it in her pocket. She wasn't sure what she had expected, but she felt . . . disappointed. *Why didn't the person sign it? They obviously don't want me to know who they are, for some reason. And who's 'all of us'?* She unscrewed the lid of the jam as if she was wringing its neck and stabbed the knife into it.

8

Walking to school with Ellie the next morning, Becca felt eyes on her. *What have I done now?* But her conscience was clear. *You're imagining it. Why would anyone be looking at you?*

They entered the playground and immediately, Rosie came over. 'I'm so sorry,' she said, putting a hand on Becca's arm.

'Have I missed something?' Becca asked.

'I don't think Becca knows, Rosie,' said Claire.

Becca frowned. 'What don't I know?'

'We're really sorry,' said Claire. 'It looks bad, but I'm sure it'll clean up.'

'What will?' Rosie bit her lip. *What could it possibly be?* 'Just tell me!'

'The book swap,' said Rosie, and Becca's heart sank. 'It's been vandalised, but it isn't too bad. I mean, they haven't set fire to it or anything.'

Ellie's grip on her hand tightened. 'What's vandalised, Mummy?'

'Don't worry, Ellie. Some silly people have messed about with the book swap, that's all.'

'*Our* book swap? Why?' Ellie gazed up at her, her eyes suspiciously shiny.

'Don't cry, Ellie. They're just silly people who don't know any better.' The bell rang, early for once, and Becca wondered if one of the staff had spotted her. 'Please don't worry, sweetheart. I'll go there now and see what needs doing.'

'The person who did it,' said Ellie, and Becca had never seen her so cross. '*They* don't know our values.' And she flounced off to the line.

***

Becca was one of the last to leave the playground that morning. Rosie and Claire had asked if she would like them to come too, but she had refused on the grounds that she was a big girl. She considered going home and making a strong cup of tea to help her face it, but she knew that if she did, she wouldn't go back. So she gritted her teeth and marched down the road.

The book swap was still standing, but the bright red was streaked with black aerosol paint. As Becca drew nearer, she saw a few windows had been smashed. Books were in a heap on the floor, some with their covers ripped off. The sign the library helpers had made lay in four jagged pieces.

'I'm so sorry,' Becca whispered. She could barely speak for the lump in her throat. She put her hand on a corner that hadn't been graffitied. *I took care of the book swap, and for what? For someone to come along and ruin it. What's the point of caring if this is what happens?*

She rubbed the paintwork slowly, then realised what she was doing and stopped. *It's just an old phone box. It can't feel. You're projecting your own feelings onto it.* Even as she thought it, anger rose in her. *Why shouldn't I? Everyone left me alone when Phil and I split up, and I turned into a mess. No – I was already a mess, thanks to Phil. If it hadn't been for Ellie...* She put her other hand on the phone box, not caring about paint or dirt. *That's why the book swap is so important to me. I know what it's like to be abandoned.*

A leaf fluttered down and landed at Becca's feet. She blinked, hard.

'Excuse me?'

Becca almost jumped out of her skin.

The speaker was a woman, perhaps in her sixties, wearing black trousers and a red blazer and holding a clipboard. Next to her stood a man about the same age in a grey suit.

'Excuse me?' the woman repeated. 'Is this a good time?'

'Does it look like a good time?' Becca replied, and

clamped her mouth shut to keep in a sob.

'Well, not really, but I take it this is the community book swap?'

Becca swallowed. 'It was until somebody vandalised it. It was absolutely fine yesterday, and now look at it.'

'You're obviously upset,' said the man.

'Yes, I am,' said Becca. 'If I find out who did it, I'll wring their neck. No, better than that.' She turned to the book swap and took a picture with her phone. 'I'll report this to the police. I'm not having it.'

'I completely understand,' said the woman. 'Would you mind answering a few questions?'

'Yes, I would. I've got a crime to report. And once the police are finished, assuming they come at all, I've got to clean this up and put everything in order.' She opened the photos app on her phone, scrolled until she found the photo she had taken of Ellie, grinning in front of the book swap, and thrust it under the woman's nose. 'There. That's what it's supposed to look like.'

'I see,' said the woman.

'Anyway, what do you want?' asked Becca. 'Are you doing a survey?'

'In a way,' said the woman. 'But we've taken up enough of your time. Thank you very much.' And she strolled off with the man.

Becca watched them go, passing a short, stout

woman on crutches, and forced herself to face the book swap again. The panes would need replacing – not to mention clearing up the broken glass – and lots of books would have to be thrown away. Maybe the library helpers wouldn't even make another sign, after what had happened.

'This is a mess and no mistake.' The woman leaned on her crutches and gazed up at the book swap. 'Who let it get like this? I hand it over for a few weeks while I get my hip sorted, and this happens.'

'It was fine until today,' said Becca. 'Someone's done this overnight.' Then the penny dropped. 'You must be Mrs—'

'Mrs Walentynowicz,' said the woman. 'Most people call me Mrs Val. I prefer that to having my name mangled. Anyway, what did you tell those two?'

'I didn't exactly tell them to mind their own business,' said Becca, 'but I might have implied it.'

'Oh dear,' said Mrs Val, grinning. 'I bet they didn't like that.'

Becca shrugged. 'Does it matter?'

'It does if you want Meadley to win Best-Kept Village. I've seen that pair round here before. They're the judges.' And as Becca stared at her in horror, Mrs Val broke into a wheezy laugh.

9

Becca hurried home, head down, cheeks burning. *Of all the times to speak your mind… When people find out, they'll probably never speak to me again. I'll be thrown out of the PTA. Hopefully Ellie won't be bullied…*

You told them the truth. And you're stressed. People will understand.

They don't usually.

'You're not thinking straight,' Phil would have said. 'You're getting emotional. Hormones.' At that point she had usually gone into another room. Otherwise she would have shouted at him in front of Ellie.

She quickened her pace until she was almost running.

Back at the flat, she made herself that strong cup of tea and looked up the police non-emergency number.

'I wish to report a crime,' she said, when the call was answered.

'Right,' said the man on the other end of the line, sounding rather impressed. 'What sort of crime?'

'Vandalism. Someone's graffitied the book swap in Meadley and smashed its windows.'

'The . . . book swap?'

'Yes. It's an old phone box near the primary school, on Beech Lane.'

A pause. 'So it's not your property.'

'No, it belongs to the community. I was hoping someone could come and – and take fingerprints?'

'Mmm. So no one was seen doing it?'

'Not as far as I know,' said Becca. 'It happened overnight.'

'Very unlikely to be CCTV down there, and not much chance of fingerprints, to be honest with you.'

'So you won't do anything?'

The man sighed. 'Of course we'd like to get an officer to the scene of every crime, however minor. It's resources, you see. What I will do is inform your local community support officer: he'll call in when he's next in the village. Can I take your name and number, please.'

Becca gave them, so quietly that the call handler had to ask again, then sat brooding.

It is a minor crime, in the scheme of things.

Yes, but it's stupid and pointless. Whoever did it

should be brought to justice.

They won't be. She closed her eyes and saw the book swap, graffitied and broken. She tried to remember it as it had been, bright, clean, and filled with interesting books, but the image was blurred as if it had never been real at all.

Will I ever be able to restore it to what it was? What if the vandals return?

You won't know unless you try. Besides, you'd better clear away that broken glass before someone cuts themselves.

Becca imagined a small child reaching towards a broken pane and immediately jumped out of her chair.

***

She was sweeping up the last of the broken glass when an irregular tapping made her look round.

'Only me,' said Mrs Val. 'Not that I can do much, but I thought you might like company. I live down the road and saw you passing. And I'm supposed to do short walks with these things. Well, my daughter said I wasn't allowed to leave the house without her. But she also said that if I did I was to use crutches.'

'Oh. Thanks.' Becca gave the floor of the book swap a final sweep, then emptied the dustpan carefully into a bag she had brought for the purpose.

'I can take that if you want,' said Mrs Val. 'Put it in my recycling bin.' Balancing carefully, she slipped the handle of the bag over the grip of her crutch.

A car stopped and the driver wound down his window. Bruce Springsteen at full volume almost blew Becca's hair back. 'What's happened?'

'Vandalism,' said Becca. 'I reported it to the police but it's low priority for them, so I'm cleaning it.'

'Got a few panes out,' said the man.

Becca sighed. 'Yes. Luckily they haven't left any jagged edges. I've just cleared up the glass.'

'My brother's a glazier, lives in Meadhurst but works here too. I'll drop him a text, see if he'll come by and look at it.' The man picked up his phone, took a picture, and typed a few words. They heard a whoosh. 'There. Well, hope you get it sorted. I'd lend a hand, but I've got to be somewhere at ten o'clock. I'll try and come down later.'

'Thank you,' said Becca, barely able to believe it. What luck that someone with the power to help them had happened to drive by. She stared after the diminishing car, misty-eyed.

'*Are* you going to clean it?' asked Mrs Val.

Becca rolled her eyes. 'That's the plan, yes.'

'What are you using?'

'I'll try vinegar, and if that doesn't work I'll have a think.' She poured vinegar on a soft cloth and began to rub the paintwork.

A few minutes later, the black paint was faded but still visible.

'Gonna be a long job,' said Mrs Val, who was

leaning on her crutches, watching. 'I reckon you need something stronger.'

'I do too,' said Becca, 'but I don't want to damage the paint. The book swap's been traumatised enough already.'

Another car pulled up and Claire got out. 'Hi Becca, how's it going?'

'Slowly,' said Becca, indicating the faded patch of spray paint.

'I might be able to help,' said Claire. 'My husband works in chemicals – solvents and things, don't know what exactly – so I asked him what would get spray paint off a phone box. He said this would probably do it.' She reached into the side bucket of her car door and held up a brightly-coloured spray bottle. 'I checked online, not that I don't trust him but just to be sure, and the internet agrees. Maybe test it on a hidden bit first.'

Becca read the back of the bottle. *Use in a well-ventilated area.* 'We're outside, anyway.' She shrugged, sprayed a tiny bit on a fresh cloth, then went to the side of the book swap furthest from the road and gave it a tentative rub. She half-expected a genie to appear.

The cloth came away filthy, revealing glossy red paint.

'Wow!' Becca had another go to make sure it wasn't a fluke. 'Thanks, Claire! You've saved me a day of scrubbing.'

'No problem,' said Claire. 'What will you do with those books?' She waved a hand at the small heap of torn, battered volumes sitting on the pavement.

'No idea,' said Becca, as she cleaned. 'I guess they'll have to be recycled.'

'One of the school mums makes book sculptures,' said Claire. 'You know, those folded thingies you sometimes see – apples and hearts and hedgehogs – made out of old books. I bet she'd take them. Maybe she'd make one for the book swap.'

'Really?' Becca considered what sort of sculpture would suit the book swap. And as she thought, another car stopped behind Claire's.

10

A man in a white shirt and suit trousers got out of the car and approached them. 'I'm Tim Jameson, from the *Meadborough and District Times*. Is one of you...' He took a phone from his pocket and consulted it. 'Becca?'

What on earth does someone from the local paper want with me? Claire nudged Becca and she raised a timid hand to shoulder level. 'That's me.'

'Oh good. I saw a post on social media about the book swap being vandalised and I decided to come and see for myself.' He inspected the phone box. 'You're doing a grand job fixing it up. It looked shocking in the photos.'

'Thank you,' said Becca. 'I've had lots of help, though. Claire brought cleaning stuff, and Mrs—' She turned to Mrs Val. 'I'm terribly sorry, could you tell the reporter your name?'

'Mrs Walentynowicz. I can spell it if you like.' She leaned on her crutch and extended a hand to the reporter, who shook it gently. 'I'm in charge of waste disposal.' She tapped the carrier bag. 'We have a glazier stopping by later.'

'Excellent,' said Tim. 'Do you mind if I take notes? And could I get a quote or two?'

'Yes, of course,' said Claire, and Becca's heart beat a little faster. *I'm going to be in the local paper.* She wasn't sure if she was more excited or apprehensive. She also wasn't sure what she thought about the possibility of Phil reading whatever they wrote. No doubt he would think her activities a waste of time. But did his opinion matter?

'Great,' said Tim. 'People should understand the importance of community assets like this. I'm planning to phone the headteacher at the primary for a quote, too.'

Claire looked past him. 'You won't need to do that, Tim. Here he comes now.'

Becca followed her gaze with interest. She hadn't actually met the headteacher of Ellie's school yet. When she had visited the school, on a tour for prospective parents booked at the last minute, the deputy head had shown them round—

She gasped. Walking towards them, in what looked like the navy suit he had worn on that fateful day, was the man who had tried to dump a bag of books at the book swap. The man who had practically run away from her. And she had made it pretty clear what she thought of him. *Oh, heck.*

'Hello, Mr Cole,' said Claire.

'Hi,' he said, smiling. 'Hello, Tim. And hello, Mrs Walentynowicz. Good to see you back.'

Becca hoped her face wasn't as red as she suspected. She glanced down at herself. Her jeans were grubby and she was wearing the final shapeless old top she had kept for cleaning, accessorised with yellow rubber gloves.

'You must be Becca,' he said. 'I'm Declan Cole, the headteacher at Meadley Primary. You're Ellie's mum, aren't you? In Mrs Shaw's class.' He offered a hand.

Becca took off her glove, wiped her hand on her jeans, and shook it. 'That's me,' she said. 'I didn't realise you were— I'm sorry I was a bit abrupt. You know, when—'

He laughed. 'I deserved it. I should have done a quality check on those books.' He turned to Tim. 'Becca does a fine job of looking after the book swap.'

Becca brushed a sweaty strand of hair off her forehead and wished the ground would swallow her up. 'Anyone could do it,' she muttered. 'And I haven't been doing it that long, anyway. Only while Mrs…' She took a deep breath and went for it. 'While Mrs

Walentynowicz was out of action.'

'I'm not sure *anyone* could take care of the book swap,' said Declan Cole. 'Even if that were true, most people don't. We need more people to take on jobs like this. Indeed, some of our pupils visited the book swap this week as part of our commitment to the school values.'

'Responsibility and community,' said Becca. 'Ellie told me.'

'There you are,' said Declan. 'This is important to the whole school, from reception onwards. Once the book swap's back to its normal self, we'll have a grand reopening. Bring the children down, cut a ribbon, get someone to do a speech…'

'Ooh yes,' said Claire. 'Maybe people could walk to school afterwards and have refreshments. Any excuse to eat cupcakes.' She grinned.

'Sounds like a plan,' said Declan. 'I daresay the paper could send a photographer.'

'For a load of cute schoolkids and a feel-good story?' said Tim. 'Absolutely.'

'You should get a photo of these three for the paper now, though,' said Declan. 'Their efforts ought to be recognised.'

'Oh no,' said Becca, before she could stop herself. 'I bet I'm a right state.'

Claire grinned at her. 'You look fine, Becca. Glowing with health.'

So I am a red sweaty mess. She pushed her hair back and sighed, then grew even warmer as she saw Declan Cole looking at her.

Tim checked his watch. 'I have an appointment in the village, so shall I return in a couple of hours? That'll give you time to freshen up.'

Becca could have hugged him. 'I'll carry on here for a bit first,' she said. 'Get the book swap ready for its close-up.' *But what a shower I'll have when I've finished.*

Mrs Walentynowicz chuckled. 'Fame at last,' she said, and swung her way slowly down the lane, the carrier bag on her crutch spinning.

'I should get back to school,' said Declan. 'Tim, if you need anything, drop me an email. Oh, and Becca...'

'Yes?' Becca paused, cloth in hand, wondering what a busy headteacher in a smart suit could possibly have to say to her.

He smiled at her. 'I'm glad you enjoyed the book.'

11

Becca strolled through the school gate and pressed the doorbell. 'I'm here for the PTA,' she said to the intercom.

'That's Becca, isn't it?' said Angie. 'Come on in.' Becca heard a buzz and pulled the door. As she walked down the corridor, she looked at the wall displays. More than one included a red phone box.

The room was perhaps half full when she arrived. 'Hi, Becca,' said Rosie, as Becca unwound her scarf. 'Ooh, is that a new top?'

Becca smiled. 'It is. Ellie said I should buy myself a treat from my first pay packet.'

Saffron came over. 'Oh yes, you're working now. How's it going?'

'Fine, thanks.'

A week or so after the book swap had appeared in the local paper, Becca was apprehended by Angie when she went into reception to collect books. 'I have a letter for you,' said Angie. 'Well, it says *Becca who runs the book swap* on it, which is good enough for me.'

Becca's brow furrowed. 'Who would send me a letter here?'

'Someone who can't reach you any other way,' said Angie. 'Go on, open it. I could use some excitement.'

Becca ripped open the envelope and found a sheet of letterheaded paper.

Dear Becca,

Please excuse me contacting you in this way, but I wasn't sure how else to reach you.

We are looking for someone to manage the Meadborough Hospice charity bookshop in Meadhurst when the current manager retires. None of the volunteers wish to step up, and when we read an article about your work with the book swap in the local newspaper, we wondered if you would be interested.

'Are they having a laugh?' said Becca.

Angie wagged a finger. 'No spoilers, please.'

We have excellent flexible-working policies and the current manager will provide training. If you wish to discuss the role, please call the number above.

Yours sincerely,
Mandy Fairweather
Bookshops Manager, Meadborough Hospice

'Am I seeing what I think I'm seeing?' asked Becca, giving Angie the letter.

Angie skimmed it. 'Looks like it,' she said, with a grin. 'You're being headhunted.'

Becca phoned, then went for an interview, full of nerves and convinced she would be laughed out of the room. When she left, she was still sure she wouldn't last two minutes once they discovered how useless she was. But she had the job, and apparently the administrative skills Phil had dismissed as fit only for dogsbody work would be invaluable.

Claire erupted into the room. 'Late to my first PTA meeting, that's a good start,' she announced, flopping down in a chair. 'I had to bring Josh and he needed a lot of settling. No Ellie, Becca?'

'No, she's sleeping over at her dad's tonight. They're probably watching a princess movie right now.'

Phil had actually phoned her two weeks before. In the evening, too, which was unprecedented. 'Becca, we don't see eye to eye about a lot of things, but I'd like to spend more time with Ellie.'

Becca raised her eyebrows. 'Taking Ellie at weekends when you're supposed to would be a start.'

A long pause. 'I'm sorry. It's hard to fit everything in, I guess. But I want you to know that I'm always there for her.' His voice was slightly thick, and Becca suspected a few beers had brought on an attack of sentimentality.

She got up and closed the door, in case Ellie wasn't asleep. 'What's brought this on?'

'Nothing. Well, um, Ariane says she isn't impressed with me as a parent and I have to do better. Certainly when we have kids together.'

Becca winced, out of habit, then realised Phil's doings didn't matter to her any more unless they affected Ellie.

'Anyway.' Another pause. 'Anyway, I'll definitely have Ellie this weekend, and for a sleepover in the week too. If that's convenient.'

Becca wondered whether Ariane was in the room, holding up cue cards. 'Ellie has an after-school club on Wednesdays and she's going to tea with a friend on Friday, but her other weeknights are free. I'll have to talk it over with Ellie first, though.'

Her first weeknight alone had felt strange, as if a vital part of her had gone missing. But she had cooked herself prawn risotto (Ellie wouldn't touch prawns), watched a romcom, and enjoyed herself tremendously.

The door opened again and Declan Cole hurried in. 'Sorry I'm late . . . got held up on a phone call.' He sat down and put his phone on silent mode.

Saffron cleared her throat and everyone looked her way. 'That's quite all right, Declan. Let's get started. Our main business, of course, is the Christmas fair. Our major players are in position, obviously, but there's the matter of the games…'

Becca volunteered to run the tombola, while Rosie plumped for hook-a-duck and Claire for the coconut shy. 'If I'm dealing with kids throwing things, I'd better stick to the non-alcoholic mulled wine,' she said ruefully.

'*You* can,' said Mrs Hanratty. 'Those of us involved in the carol concert may well indulge.'

The remaining stalls were settled, a winning design chosen for the cover of the carol-concert programme, and progress reports given on the technology update and the year six French exchange. 'Any other business?' asked Saffron.

'I have,' said Becca. 'The school's adoption of the book swap is featured as a case study on the Best-Kept Village website, and also on several platforms encouraging young readers.'

'Was that from your press release?' asked Saffron.

'I believe so,' replied Becca. 'Thanks for sending me a template. It helped a lot.'

'Any time,' said Saffron, inclining her head graciously.

'I take it everything is running smoothly, now that

you've gone part-time at the book swap?' said Declan.

'Yes, it is. The volunteer rota is working really well and the book swap social-media feeds are getting lots of views. Mrs Walentynowicz is posting at least once a day on Twitter, Facebook, and Instagram, and she's shared the password with the volunteer team for us to post too.'

Declan laughed. 'She never ceases to surprise me.'

Saffron leaned forward. 'Anything else to add, anyone? No? In that case, let's wrap up. I need to be on with Chicago in twenty minutes.'

Everyone got up and began putting on coats. 'Want a lift, Becca?' asked Claire.

'I'm fine, thanks,' Becca replied. 'It's a nice night for a walk. It's such a change to go anywhere without a little hand pulling me forward or back.'

Claire grimaced. 'Tell me about it.'

As people dispersed, Becca wrote a couple of reminders in her pocket notebook, then stood up and reached for her coat. Declan was still sitting at the table, typing on his phone. Everyone else had left.

'I thought that went well,' said Becca.

He looked up. 'Yes, it did. Lots of progress.' He put his phone down. 'Um...'

'Could I ask you a question?'

His eyebrows knitted slightly. 'Er, yes?'

'That note you left me, at the book swap. Why didn't you sign it?'

He fiddled with his phone. Then he met her eyes, and to her surprise his cheeks were slightly pink. 'I suppose... It's a bit silly.'

'Go on. I won't laugh.'

'Well, as I was writing the note, in haste as usual, it started sounding more and more official. Really headteachery, and I didn't want to come across that way. I have enough of that here, at school.'

Becca smiled. 'I imagine you do.' She paused, studying him. 'So why did you admit it was you? You didn't have to.'

'Because it felt dishonest. I mean, who leaves anonymous notes? And besides, I like meeting people who enjoy the same sort of books as I do. What's the point of hiding?'

'Exactly,' said Becca. *That's what I was doing. Hiding in my flat, scared to engage with anything or anyone in case I got hurt again. And it took a battered old phone box to drag me out of it.* 'What's your favourite Terry Pratchett book?' she asked, to lighten the mood.

'Not sure. I tend to prefer the Sam Vimes ones.'

'My favourite characters so far are Tiffany Aching and Nanny Ogg,' said Becca.

'I'm not surprised. We should have a proper book chat sometime.'

Becca half-expected him to get up from his chair, to say that he had a report to write or policies to review, or whatever headteachers did, but he didn't. He stayed sitting there, looking at her. 'Ellie's at a sleepover tonight,' she said. 'So if you wanted to, I don't know, go for a coffee somewhere and talk books...'

'My kids are at their mum's during the week,' said Declan. 'There's a country pub on the road to Meadhurst that does good coffee, if you're OK with that? I can drop you off afterwards.'

'Sure,' said Becca. She could barely hear herself over the thudding of her racing heart.

In no time at all they were in Declan's car, driving silently out of the gates. Declan turned into Beech Lane. 'Those solar lights are doing well,' he said.

Ahead of them, the windows of the book swap glowed with warm light. It stood in a carpet of bright leaves, looking as if it had travelled from another place.

As they passed, Becca saw the neat rows of books waiting to be read. With the hand furthest from Declan, she gave the book swap a little wave, and watched it in the wing mirror until it was a bright dot in the distance.

Bonus Item:
Make your own book hedgehog!

I made one of these a while ago, when one of my kids was poorly and I was looking for something low-pressure that we could do together. They're surprisingly easy to make and they look quite impressive. I made one for the library of the primary school I tutor at, and he's become a library mascot!

There are several free how-to guides on the web, all with a slightly different way of making your book hog. What follows is what I did (and I'm not great at crafts).

You will need:

An old, knackered paperback book you don't want any more. This can be quite short – say 100 pages.

Something to make the eyes, nose and feet. I had a black foam sheet, but you could use card. And if you have any googly eyes, you know what to do.

Scissors and glue (PVA works well).

Method:

Fold the first page in half lengthways, so that the outer edge of the page is as close to the spine as you can get it. Then fold the top and bottom corners right into the middle, again as close to the spine as you can, so each corner forms a right-angled triangle. This will start to form the body of the hog. Some guides say you have to fold the pages all one way, or change direction part way. I don't think it matters, so I fold all the pages the same way.

Continue folding pages until you have a nice tightly packed semicircle of hog. It will get a bit trickier as the body of the hog grows.

If you haven't already, take off the book covers. Tear off any pages you don't need.

Put one piece of the book cover under your hog and draw round it. Then cut it out, cutting inside the line so that the cardboard won't show on the finished hog.

If you're adding feet, draw some on your foam/card and cut them out. I don't think you need more than two. Put the bit of book cover you've just cut out under your hog, slip the feet into position, and stick the back part of the foot to the book cover. Then stick the book cover onto the bottom of the hog, with the feet between the book cover and the hog.

Cut out and affix eyes and nose in the relevant places.

You can also add ears. I cut out a couple of small teardrop shapes from a spare leaf of the book, then pinched the top of the teardrop in half and stuck each ear between a couple of the folded leaves, above and a little way out from each eye.

And that's it! Behold your book hedgehog! Though you might want to let the glue dry first...

The Postbox Topper

1

'I'm so glad you decided to come tonight,' said Vix.

'Mmm.' Julie concentrated on picking her way along the pavement while Vix sailed on ahead, occasionally stopping for her to catch up. The path to the library wasn't well lit at the best of times, and she was worried about frost and slippery patches.

'I'm sure you'll enjoy Hooked on Yarn. Everyone does – I can't wait for Thursdays. There are older people too: not just my age. It's a shame you haven't been before.'

'I don't think I was in the right frame of mind,' Julie replied.

'No, I suppose not, what with— But it'll do you good to start going out again.' Vix gave her a friendly pat on the arm. 'It must be, what, eighteen months?'

'Nearly two years.'

'Gosh, time flies, doesn't it? Not that— Anyway,

here we are.' Vix ushered Julie in. 'This is the library.'

'I do live in Meadley, you know, and I use the library.' She popped in most weekends to borrow books, usually mysteries, and would often chat to the librarian on duty.

Vix sailed towards the desk. 'This is my friend Julie. She's coming to Hooked on Yarn.'

Corinne, who often chatted to Julie about the last book she had borrowed, raised her eyebrows. 'Hooked on Yarn, eh?'

'I've probably forgotten everything I ever knew about knitting,' said Julie. 'And I never learned to crochet. But I'm willing to give it a go, and Vix assures me I'll enjoy it.'

'I'm sure you will,' said Corinne, smiling. 'You know the way, Vix.'

'Yes, let's go through.' Vix shepherded Julie towards the space to the side of the main library which was used for talks and activities. Today, the tables had been pushed into the middle and sitting around them was a group of women, unpacking balls of yarn from their bags and chatting.

'Hello, everyone!' cried Vix. 'I've brought a new recruit. This is Julie. We work together.'

'Hi, Julie,' said a fortysomething woman with winged glasses and a long brown bob. Julie was sure she'd seen her in the village coffee shop, reading. She was wearing a red and white striped sweater appliquéd with knitted navy flowers. Julie wondered how on earth she washed it without the colours running. 'I'm Lucy. Are you local?'

'Yes, I live on Beech Lane, near the primary school. I've lived in Meadley for three years.'

'Ahhh, you're an incomer, then.' She grinned. 'Not that I believe in all that snobby "My family have been here for generations" rubbish, but you know what some people are like.'

'Idiots,' said a young woman with pink hair and a T-shirt which proclaimed *KNITTING NEEDLES ARE A WEAPON*. 'I'm Tegan, by the way.'

'Hello, Tegan.' Julie peered at the mass of pink wool dangling from Tegan's crochet hook. 'What are you making?'

'It's a uterus,' said Tegan. 'Anatomically correct. It's an art piece.'

'Tegan's our resident angry young woman,' said Vix, grinning. 'Aren't you, Tegan?'

'I don't see why crocheting a uterus makes me an angry person,' said Tegan, looking mutinous. 'I mean, obviously it isn't just *any* uterus—'

A woman in a Peruvian jacket rushed in and flung herself into the nearest chair. 'Sorry I'm late: I was dealing with a tantrum at home. For some reason, Jake now can't eat anything that's touched another type of food on the plate. Not good when you've given them fish fingers and chips with peas and sweetcorn.'

Tegan looked horrified. 'Don't tell me you had to separate the peas from the sweetcorn, Natalie.'

Natalie shrugged. 'What do you think?'

'Female oppression,' muttered Tegan.

The woman sitting at the far corner of the table cleared her throat. 'As everyone's here, shall we get on?' She was somewhere in her thirties, with cropped dark hair and a chunky sweater. Julie wondered if she'd made it herself.

Various nods, and murmurs of 'Yes, Miriam.' Even Tegan put down her crochet and paid attention. *We have a group leader,* thought Julie.

'I've been thinking,' said Miriam. 'We did really well with our crocheted poppies for Remembrance Day, and then the stall at the Christmas fair. Maybe we could do a project together. Something for the village.'

'How do you mean?' asked Vix.

'I know what we could do,' said Tegan. 'Yarn bombing.'

'Yarn bombing?' Vix laughed. 'What the heck is that?'

'When you knit covers for bollards,' said Tegan. 'And wrap lamp posts and trees and... Stuff like that. Guerilla knitting.'

'Ooh, I've never knitted a gorilla,' said a trim woman with short grey hair and smiling eyes.

Tegan laughed. 'Hang on, Bernie, I'll show you.' She pulled out her phone, and after a bit of searching, held it up.

Julie saw a tree with its trunk and branches wrapped in red and green squares. Baubles dangled from woollen chains. 'That looks complicated,' she said, faintly.

'Don't worry, Jules,' said Vix. 'You could do a couple of squares, I'm sure. Anyway, that's a Christmas one, and it's almost February.'

'That was just an example,' said Tegan. 'We could make a difference. We could knit big stand-up arrows and point them at the potholes. Or knit a life-size version of our MP and put him in the stocks.'

'Or we could start with something a bit smaller,' said Miriam. 'Like a postbox topper.'

'Oh yes, those are cool,' said Natalie. 'I've seen them on the internet. There was a snowman one in Meadhurst at Christmas.'

'What do the rest of you think?' said Miriam.

'It's a bit tame,' said Tegan. 'We could do something really radical.'

'Which would probably be taken down,' said Miriam, 'Why don't we do something people will like, and go from there?'

Tegan thought this over. 'I suppose,' she said, with a sigh. 'I do get what you mean, but . . . it's annoying.'

'I know,' Miriam soothed. 'Does anyone have any

other ideas for a group project?'

'I'm still tempted by the gorilla,' said Bernie, 'but a postbox topper seems a good idea. It's just like doing a round hat, isn't it, and then decorating it?'

'That's it,' said Miriam. 'OK, let's pick a theme, then we can look at our supplies and get started.' Julie suspected making a postbox topper had been Miriam's intention all along.

Miriam's eyes met hers and she jumped. 'Julie – it is Julie, isn't it?'

'That's right,' said Julie. She felt unaccountably nervous.

Miriam smiled at her. 'Are you a knitter or a crocheter?'

'I'm not sure I'm either,' said Julie. 'I never learnt to crochet, but I can knit a bit.'

'I'll get someone to take you under their wing.'

Five minutes later, Julie had been handed over to Lucy, who supplied her with a ball of wool and a crochet hook and instructed her on how to make a chain. 'After all,' she said, 'you won't know whether you prefer knitting or crochet until you've tried them both.'

'Did you make the flowers on your jumper?' asked Julie, pausing in her battle to keep the yarn on her hook and the links of the chain the same size.

'I did. And the jumper.' Lucy put her head on one side. 'I'm surprised I haven't seen you about, since you're local.'

'I work in Meadborough, so I'm not around during the day.'

'Oh,' said Lucy, and left it at that, for which Julie was grateful. 'It's nice that you found us.'

'Well, Vix brought me.' Julie felt her face grow warm. *You sound like a child who has to be taken places*, she thought to herself. *Honestly, Julie.*

'Yes, but you still came.' Lucy put down the blanket square she was crocheting and gently inspected Julie's chain. 'That's pretty good. Want to learn something else?'

Julie found herself smiling. 'Yes, if that's OK.'

Lucy laughed. 'Of course it is!'

Someone touched Julie's shoulder and she jumped. 'Are you getting on all right?' asked Vix, her brown eyes round with concern. 'I'm sorry, I would have come over before, but I couldn't get away. Catching up, you know.' From her needles dangled a blue and white striped sock sized for a very large foot.

'I – I think so.' Julie looked at Lucy for confirmation.

'She's doing really well, Vix,' said Lucy.

Vix crouched next to Julie and put a hand on her arm. 'You're sure? You don't feel overwhelmed or anything?'

'I'm fine,' said Julie, wishing Vix would disappear.

'Oh good! I'm so pleased! I wasn't sure how you'd

get on, seeing as you don't get out much. Well done you.' Vix beamed at her. 'Better go, Bernie wants a word.' And Vix strode off, the sock bobbing up and down on its needles as if it was walking too.

Some time later, as Julie was embarking on crocheting a ring, Miriam clapped her hands. 'Sorry to be schoolmarmy, but I've been doing a stocktake of the yarn cupboard. We have lots of pale green, various shades of yellow, a fair bit of white and a ball each of various other colours. We're completely out of red after doing all those poppies, obviously. Does anyone have any bright ideas? I mean, we could buy more yarn, but I like the idea of using what we have.'

'Green and yellow,' said Bernie, meditatively. 'A fruit bowl with apples and bananas?'

'We could do an abstract,' said Tegan. 'Then anything goes.'

'We could,' said Miriam, who looked as if her patience was being tested. 'But as this is our first postbox topper, it's important that people can tell what it is.'

Julie eyed the flowers on Lucy's jumper and raised her hand to the level of her shoulder. 'We could, um, maybe do something with spring flowers? A green cover, with daffodils and daisies and . . . other ones.'

'Yes!' said Natalie. 'And rabbits.'

'And crocuses,' said Lucy.

Tegan sighed. 'I suppose you want to put a rainbow

and fluffy clouds on it too, or spring lambs.'

'Definitely lambs,' said Miriam. 'Right, who's in favour of a spring-themed postbox topper?'

Everyone except Tegan raised their hand.

Tegan surveyed the group, rolled her eyes and raised hers too. 'We should do a witchy one for Halloween,' she said.

'I have no objection,' said Miriam, 'so long as it's a majority vote.'

A knock on the wall made everyone turn their heads. 'Sorry to interrupt,' said Corinne, 'but I'm closing in five minutes.' She surveyed them. 'You're very pleased with yourselves. Have you been plotting?'

Everyone looked blank. 'Us, plotting?' said Miriam. 'You must be thinking of some other group of women.'

Corinne's eyes narrowed. 'Whatever it is, it'll have to wait until next week.'

'It won't,' said Miriam. 'Everyone, decide what you'd like to crochet and put it in the WhatsApp group. Now, we'd better pack up. Needles down, folks.'

'So there's a WhatsApp group?' said Julie, as she and Vix picked their way along the path.

'Yes, shall I add you?'

'Um… I'm not on WhatsApp.'

'Oh,' said Vix. 'Never mind, I can keep you up to

speed. We see each other almost every day at work, don't we?'

'Yes, of course,' said Julie, and resolved to get WhatsApp onto her phone when she got home. That, and find a YouTube tutorial on how to crochet flowers.

2

Natalie: *I'm doing two lambs and a five-bar gate. If I can, I'll wire the lambs so they're jumping over it.*

Lucy: *I'll have a go at some daffodils. Is it cheating if we wire the stems? Or do I just do the heads?*

Bernie: *I'll do the bonnet. Seeing as gorillas aren't native to this county :(*

Tegan: *If I knit battery hens you'll complain, so I'll do ducks.*

Miriam: *Lovely, it's all coming together. Who's left, and what do you want to do?*

Vix: *I'll make cute yellow chicks. Jules, what about you? Could you do crocuses?*

Julie put down her phone. This was what she had been dreading. She could hear her heart thumping. *I have no idea where to start.* Then she realised that if she said nothing, Vix and the others might take that as agreement. She picked up the phone and began to type. *I think I can crochet some simple daisies, if that's OK. I have a ball of white wool so I only need yellow. I'm not ready for crocuses yet.*

Vix: *I'm sure someone could teach you to do a crocus next meeting. Or I could show you in our lunch breaks.*
Miriam: *Daisies would be great, Julie. I'll take on the crocuses. Vix, can you pass on yellow wool to Julie?*

OK, Julie replied. She was about to close the app when a thought struck her. After a bit of clicking, she found the group's details. There was a mute option, which she clicked. *There. If someone from the group asks, I can always say I don't check my phone very often, or that I must have muted it by accident.* She closed her eyes and exhaled, then got up and put the kettle on.

She had told Vix at work that she would make her own way to the group next time. 'It's out of your way, Vix, and I'll be quite safe walking. The road's well lit.'

'Are you sure?' said Vix. 'No one's really safe anywhere. The things you hear about that happen in broad daylight—'

'I'll be fine,' said Julie.

On the evening of the meeting Julie got ready in good time, dressing warmly, with sensible shoes. She packed her crochet hook, yarn and the daisies she had made already in a little pouch. She was locking up when the front door of the adjoining cottage opened and her neighbour Neil appeared. 'Hello Julie, off out?' His longish, unruly brown hair made him look rather like a curious lion.

'I am, as it happens.' Julie tried the handle of her door, just to be sure. Of course, it was locked.

'Going somewhere nice?'

'Yes, to a knitting and crochet group at the library.' The cuff of Neil's baggy green jumper was coming undone. Julie wondered whether she should suggest he accompany her to get it fixed.

Neil's eyebrows knitted in a humorous frown. 'Knitting and crochet? Isn't that what grannies do?'

Julie considered how to reply. There were so many things she could say, none particularly polite. 'I'm in my fifties, Neil. Maybe I'm just getting in early.'

His smile vanished. 'Oh no, I didn't mean— What I meant was that you're not old enough for that sort of thing.'

'I enjoy it. It's nice to chat to people.'

'You could chat to me,' said Neil. 'I'm only next door, if you want a conversation.'

What on earth would we talk about? thought Julie.

Whether the fence needs repainting? The state of Meadley's roads? Offers at the local supermarket?
'Thanks, Neil, I'll remember that. Anyway, must get on.'

'When will you be back?' asked Neil. 'So I can check you're home safe.'

'I'm not likely to go missing, Neil!' Julie laughed. 'And I doubt I'll get lost.' She raised a hand in farewell and walked down the path. *What a fuss over a trip to the library. Anyone would think I was off around the world.*

***

She arrived at the library to find Vix standing outside. Vix waved frantically. '*There* you are!'

Julie checked her watch. 'It's five to, Vix. I'm early.'

'Yes, well, I worry. Let's go in.' She steered Julie through the door and straight into the meeting space as if Julie might break free and make a run for it. 'Here she is!' she announced, then took the nearest chair and began unpacking her bag.

Julie was somewhat dismayed to see that everyone had made considerable progress with their parts of the project. Natalie had two lambs propped up in front of her and was working on a third. Lucy had a row of daffodils. Tegan had knitted a duck and drake with menacing, beady eyes, and a pair of ducklings swam along the table behind them. Bernie was hard at work on what looked like an enormous beret.

'Hello, Julie,' said Miriam, setting down her crochet. 'There's a spare seat over by Bernie.'

'Oh, Jules can squish in next to me,' said Vix, scraping her chair. But Julie was already making her way round the table. She sat down, put her bag on her lap and pulled out the pouch. 'They aren't great,' she said apologetically, 'but I've made a start.' She set out the daisies.

'Oh, they're cute,' said Lucy. 'And very regular. When I first began crocheting, everything began really tight then loosened until it was twice the size.'

Julie peered at everyone else's creations. 'Should I do bigger ones?' she asked. 'I wasn't sure what size to make, so I went small to be on the safe side.'

'You could do,' said Miriam. 'So long as they're not the same size as the lambs.'

'Although you'd be making a great point about GM crops,' said Tegan, and Lucy sighed.

There was much less conversation than at the previous meeting, because people were focused on their work. In some ways that was nice, thought Julie. It was relaxing not to have to think of small talk or reply to questions she found difficult, even if they weren't meant to be. Being social without being social.

An hour in, a chair scraped and everyone looked up. Miriam was inspecting the table. 'Wow,' she said,

'We're practically there. The topper itself is done, we've got lambs, a gate, ducks, chicks and lots of flowers. It'll be spectacular.'

'If you whizz the completed bits my way,' said Bernie, 'I'll arrange them on the topper, ready for sewing.'

Julie reflected on how nice it was to have someone else monitoring a project for a change, then stared as various woollen items shot past her. 'It can't be finished,' she said.

Miriam grinned. 'It's amazing what we can do when we put our minds to it.'

Bernie was arranging their contributions on the topper, which was in shades of green with a blue pond in the middle. 'Lovely,' she said. 'Can you pass me your daisies, Julie?'

Julie picked up her flowers and handed them to Bernie. Pushing them across the table as the others had done felt rude. 'I'll finish the one I'm on,' she said, and continued to crochet.

A few minutes later, Bernie clapped her hands. 'Everyone happy?'

'Oh yes,' said Miriam. 'I think you're ready to sew.'

Julie finished her daisy, worked in the end and looked up. What she saw already seemed complete. The topper was bordered with flowers. Ducks swam in the pond, chicks roamed the fields and the lambs watched one of their number hurdle a five-bar gate. 'That's amazing,' she said. 'I don't suppose you need this daisy.'

'Always room for one more,' said Bernie. She held out her hand for the daisy and put it between a daffodil and a crocus.

'Are you all right to make it up, Bernie?' asked Miriam. 'Once that's done, we can put it on.' She leaned forward and lowered her voice. 'Under cover of darkness.'

Lucy laughed. 'Is that necessary?'

Tegan tutted. 'The whole point of yarn bombing is that it's secret. It comes in the night, when no one expects it.'

Natalie giggled. 'I can see the papers. *The village was ambushed by three fluffy lambs, some chicks and a flock of evil ducks.*'

Bernie stood up and took a picture of the laid-out topper with her phone. 'There, now I've got something to work with. I reckon I can get this done tonight, if I push.'

'Let me know when you have,' said Miriam. 'If you don't mind, I'll pick it up and pop it on once the village is quiet. I doubt anyone will be out past midnight on a school night, and it would be great to get it on for the weekend. I'll put a message in the WhatsApp group when it's in place.'

Vix insisted on walking Julie home. 'Aren't you

glad I persuaded you to come to the group now?' she asked.

Julie smiled. 'Yes, it's nice. Although... Is it always so full on?'

'It can be busy,' said Vix. 'That's part of the fun.'

I suppose it is, thought Julie. *If you like that sort of thing.* She had spent so much time in the last few years struggling to stay calm and not be upset that voluntarily stepping into a busy environment seemed strange.

'Here we are,' said Vix, as they arrived at Julie's gate. 'Home sweet home.'

'Um, yes,' said Julie. 'Thanks for walking me home. You really didn't have to.'

She opened the gate and started down the path. The gate clicked to, and shortly afterwards Neil's front door opened. 'Returned from your knitting, then,' he said, leaning against the doorframe.

'I was crocheting,' said Julie. 'But yes.'

He waved a dismissive hand. 'Knitting, crocheting, isn't it the same?'

'It certainly is not,' snapped Vix, from the gate.

Neil drew back slightly. 'Sorry I spoke. You carry on doing whatever it is you've been doing. Don't mind me.'

'We've been doing something to benefit the village,' said Vix, drawing herself up.

'Oh yes? What would that be?'

'Never you mind,' Vix retorted. 'See you tomorrow, Jules.' She flounced off, chin in the air.

Neil snorted. 'Jules? That's a new one.'

'No one else calls me that,' said Julie, though she checked the road first to make sure Vix was too far away to hear. 'She's a work colleague.'

'Lucky you,' said Neil. 'If that's who you meet at this knitting club, I'm glad I'm not a member.'

Julie's skin prickled with irritation. 'You didn't have to come out and ask questions. Now, if you don't mind, I'm going in. It was quite a busy meeting.'

'Needles flying, were they?' Neil looked down at his own sweater.

'We're working on a project, actually.'

'Which is?' Neil ran a hand through his mop of curly hair. In Julie's opinion, it needed cutting. Jason would never have let his get as far as his collar.

She was tempted to echo Vix and say *Never you mind*, but the thought of following in Vix's footsteps put her off. 'You'll find out soon,' she said, instead. 'Good night, Neil.'

'Good night,' he said, as she found her key and put it in the lock. 'Jules.' And before she could reply, he closed his door.

***

The next morning, Julie left for work slightly early, so that she could drive through the village and see the postbox topper. It was hard to miss. Even at ten past eight in the morning, three people were standing by the postbox, two with dogs, gesturing and talking. She would have liked to park the car and have a proper look, but there wasn't time. Nevertheless, a glimpse of the postbox topper, with its spring lambs and bright flowers, was more than enough to make her smile all the way to work. *I helped make that,* she thought. *I can admire it at the weekend.*

Or so she thought.

She was eating a sandwich at her desk after a morning of chasing project outputs when Vix burst in. 'I don't believe it!' she cried.

Julie froze, mid-chew. 'What is it? Is something wrong in the sales department? Don't tell me the systems are playing up ag—'

'Not sales.' Vix waved her phone. 'Haven't you seen Miriam's message?'

'No, I keep my phone on silent.' Julie fumbled in her handbag.

'Here.' Vix tapped at her phone, then shoved the screen under Julie's nose.

Unbelievable, the message read. *Less than 12 hours after I put the topper on, it's vanished. Someone must have pinched it.*

'Vandals,' said Vix. 'What a waste. The work we put in to get it done, too. I'm heading to the cafeteria to eat something naughty. Want to come?'

Julie indicated her sandwich. 'I'm a bit pushed for

time, Vix—'

'In that case, I'll let you get on.' Vix stomped off and automatically Julie took another bite of her sandwich. Now, though, it had no taste at all.

3

By two o'clock, Julie was fuming.

She wasn't sure why she felt so strongly about the postbox topper. She had gone from thinking *Honestly, some people* to *Why?* to actual rage. She sat at her desk, too furious even to concentrate on the report which her boss, Greg, had dumped on her desk, and which she was supposed to be checking for errors. Not that it was her job – she was a project coordinator, not a proofreader – but Greg always wheedled that she was so good at it that he didn't trust anyone else. The report had arrived with a sticky note on the front, on which was scrawled *Work your magic, pretty please ;-) G.*

She glanced at her half-eaten sandwich, curling at the edges, then got out her phone and unmuted the WhatsApp group.

Unsurprisingly, there was a string of replies under

Miriam's post.

Lucy: *I don't believe it! It's been up all of five minutes.*
Vix: *I know! What a shocker!*
Bernie: *What do we do? Do we make another one?*
Tegan: *What's the point? They'll probably steal that too. And you lot wonder why I get angry.*
Miriam: *We probably shouldn't jump to conclusions. Maybe someone took it off for a good reason. But I must admit that I'm annoyed.*

Julie found herself taking deep breaths to calm down. She could feel tears pricking at the back of her eyes and a lump forming in her throat. *Don't be ridiculous, Julie*, she told herself. *Why are you getting upset about a bit of wool?*

It wasn't just a bit of wool, though, was it? We put effort into that. Care. Some of us might have put love into it. And someone's taken it without a second thought.

Another message popped up.

Bernie: *You'll think I'm silly, but this makes me really sad.*
Tegan: *This is why we can't do nice things.*

Julie made a strange noise. *These people are the closest thing I've had to friends since – since—* She rubbed her eyes fiercely. You couldn't call a couple of knitting sessions a friendship. Vix was her best friend now, really.

She had had friends, of course, back in Barking. Then Jason had come home one night looking as if he would burst. 'Which do you want first?' he asked. 'The good news or the bad news?'

'The bad news,' Julie said, automatically. She would always rather have the bad news first and get it over with. If the good news wasn't great, at least it wouldn't make her feel worse.

He gave her a serious look. 'Are you sure?'

She shrugged. 'You know me.'

He grinned. Perhaps the bad news wouldn't be too bad. 'They're talking about downsizing the plant.'

Julie stared at him. 'Oh no. Your job isn't affected, is it?'

'It could be. Anyway, here's the good news. I heard on the grapevine that they'll be offering voluntary redundancies and relocations.' A spark danced in his blue eyes.

'What are you thinking?' she asked, suspiciously.

'Well, I considered voluntary redundancy, but I haven't been there long enough to have much of a package.'

'Ha ha.'

'Give over!' He chuckled. 'So I had a look at the locations of the other plants. Loads are in the back of beyond, but there's one a few miles from a place called Meadborough which could be a good fit. They have product lines similar to the one I manage, but bigger, and they make more stuff. Chances are that I might get asked to relocate there anyway, but I figured I should make the first move.'

Julie stared at him. 'Where the heck is Meadborough? What about my job? What am I supposed to do?'

'It's a nice little market town with surrounding villages, set in beautiful countryside. The sort of place we've always talked about retiring to one day. Here.' He pulled out his phone. 'There's a Wikipedia entry. Look at those hills. We could bike around the countryside together. No more London traffic.'

'I don't have a bike.'

'You could get one. Just think about it. It could be the best thing we've ever done. Meadborough has a mainline station to London, so we wouldn't be cut off from the outside world.'

'OK, I'll think about it,' said Julie.

But following that first conversation, things moved quickly. As it turned out, Jason's division was closing much earlier than he had anticipated. A month later, he had interviewed for and got an equivalent role at the Meadborough plant, and a month after that, the removal van arrived at their flat.

'From a flat to a house, eh?' Jason said, pulling her close. 'What about that?'

Jason revelled in their new home, a terraced cottage in the village of Meadley. He went for long bike rides, joined a cycling club, sampled the craft beer at his new local.

'I hardly see you nowadays,' Julie said one night, when he returned from the village.

'It's the time of year,' he said. 'There's always lots going on at Christmas. You're always welcome to come along. Lots of the cycling wives do.'

'Cycling widows, you mean. It's not really my scene. I don't fancy sitting in the corner with a glass of white wine while you talk about pedals and cleats and whether you should shave your legs or not. And before you ask, no, you shouldn't. Anyway, there's the house to get straight. Rooms to paint, stuff to fix. Plus I don't understand how the contents of our flat don't fit in an actual house. I swear it's a reverse Tardis: smaller on the inside.'

'I can always take some bits and bobs to work,' he said, 'now I've got an office of my own.'

That was where Jason had died the following September. The caretaker had come round to lock up and found him, cold and sagging in his chair. A ruptured aneurysm in his brain, according to the post-mortem. There was no way anyone could have known, since Jason had always been fit as a fiddle and had had no symptoms. *If you'd had headaches,* thought Julie, *or double vision, or anything that could have told us...*

Julie considered selling up and returning to Barking. That seemed an impossibly big task. She'd have to find a smaller flat, her post in Barking had been filled, and she had a job in Meadborough. More to the point, she couldn't face another upheaval.

She kept going to work: she found the dull routine comforting. Maintain spreadsheets, police milestones, nudge people until things got done. Besides, she'd worked at the company for less than a year. If she went missing for a few weeks, she might return to find that she had no job at all. When she came home, though, to a house now too big for her, she made a cup of tea and sank into an armchair, too sad and weary to do anything. Usually, the tea went cold. *This isn't how it was supposed to be*, she whispered sometimes.

And the friends she had promised to keep in touch with, who had sworn they would keep in touch with her? Mostly Julie let the phone ring when they called, unable to face another outpouring of sympathy, and she took herself out of cheery group chats. Gradually, because she wasn't part of their plans any more, the texts stopped coming too, except at Christmas and birthdays. Oh, and the anniversary of Jason's death.

Thinking of you xxx

In that respect, Vix had been kinder than she deserved.

She had been sitting in the cafeteria, poking at her plate of macaroni cheese and feeling thoroughly miserable, when someone said 'Mind if I join you?'

A tall, broad woman who Julie vaguely remembered from her induction was standing there with a tray. 'I'm Vix. You're Julie, aren't you?'

'That's right.'

Vix nodded towards Julie's plate. 'That looks nice.'

Julie shrugged. 'It's OK. It saves cooking at night.' She wasn't lazy and she was a reasonable cook, but the thought of planning meals for one, or cooking the quantities she always had and freezing a portion, was too depressing for words.

'I heard about your husband,' said Vix. 'I'm so sorry. What a thing to happen.'

'It was,' said Julie. 'It was terrible.' All of a sudden she was crying.

Vix banged down her tray and put an arm round her. 'It's OK, Julie. You let it out. It's fine.'

Since then, Vix had always made a point of checking in on her and making sure she was all right. She lived at the other end of Meadley with her partner, Dave, and while she wasn't exactly who Julie would have chosen for a friend, she had been very kind.

But now, for the first time in a long time, Julie felt as if she had friends.

She blinked, and looked at her phone screen. WhatsApp was still open. Before she knew it, she was typing a message.

Whoever did this ought to be ashamed of themselves. I'm going to track them down and get the postbox topper back.

Great idea! Vix responded, almost immediately.

Miriam replied perhaps a minute later. *It's good of you to suggest it, Julie, but how?*

I've read more mystery and detective books than I've had hot dinners, Julie typed. *I'll find a way.* She thought for a moment, then added: *I have my methods, Watson.*

Go Sherlock! posted Lucy.

Right, thought Julie, *I will.*

She made a list of people who might possibly steal a postbox topper. It wasn't very specific.

A jobsworth postal worker
Kids doing it for a laugh
Someone who's jealous of it

Who could that be? Julie frowned. *A disgruntled local knitter?*

How could she know for sure who had taken it? It wasn't as if anyone had been watching the postbox.

Surely anyone who had seen someone remove the topper would report it.

With that in mind, she rang the parish council. She didn't expect an answer, but within two rings there was a click and a friendly voice said 'Hello, Meadley Parish Council, Clerk of the Council speaking.'

'Oh, hello,' said Julie. 'I'm calling about the postbox topper that's gone missing.'

'Oh yes, I heard about the postbox topper. You say it's gone missing?'

Julie sighed. 'I don't need to ask my next question, then. I wondered if anyone had reported seeing it being taken.'

'I'm afraid not. When did this happen?'

'It had gone by one o'clock.' Miriam's message reporting the topper missing had been timestamped *12:56.*

'In that case, definitely not. I checked the answerphone when I came back from lunch. There were no messages, and you're the first person who's said anything about it. I'd suggest looking at the CCTV in the middle of the village—'

'Oh, is there CCTV?' Julie exclaimed.

'There is, but it doesn't cover the postbox. I'm really sorry, I don't think I can help.'

'Thanks for your time. I'll see what the police can do.'

'I'm not sure—' But Julie had already ended the

call.

'Good afternoon, Meadborough constabulary.'

'I wish to report... I'm not sure if it's theft or vandalism.'

The voice on the other end of the phone sounded amused. 'Surely you must know, madam.'

'A postbox topper has been stolen from the postbox in Meadley village.'

'A postbox topper.' A pause. 'What would that be?'

'You must have seen them. It's a sort of knitted hat that goes on top of a postbox. This one was decorated in a spring theme, with animals and flowers on.'

'Right.' Another pause. 'Well, you learn something every day. So this is a hat for a postbox.'

'Yes.'

'Made of wool.'

'Yes, made of wool.'

'So presumably not of high value.'

'The wool isn't, but a great deal of work went into it and—'

'I really don't think this is a matter for the police, madam. We can barely keep up with proper criminals.'

'I might have known you'd say that,' Julie said bitterly.

'If you leave your number, madam, I'll keep it on file. Then if any of our officers spot a suspicious character wearing a large spring-themed hat, we can take the appropriate action and let you know.'

Julie ended the call and slammed her phone on the desk. Then she turned it to silent mode, put it in her bag, and picked up the report she had been neglecting.

At five o'clock, having read the same page of the report several times, Julie left the office and drove to Meadley. However, she didn't go straight home. Instead, she parked in the village car park and walked round to the postbox. Unsurprisingly, it stood a few feet from the post office, which was in the middle of a small parade of shops. *Why didn't anyone see?*

She looked this way and that. A small alley ran between two of the shops – where did it lead? She walked over and peered down it, but it ended in a padlocked wooden gate. *That's a dead end, unless whoever took it has a key.* The alley divided the hardware shop and the grocer's. *Why would either of them want it?*

She turned and almost bumped into Neil. 'Sorry,' he said, then realised who she was. 'Hello. Why were you peeking in there?'

'The postbox topper our group made has been stolen,' said Julie. 'I'm trying to work out who did it.'

'The postbox topper?' Neil looked at her, then swung round to gaze at the postbox. 'Oh, I see!' He grinned. 'So that was your top-secret project?'

'It was,' Julie said, stiffly. 'Until someone pinched it. It had only been on the postbox for a few hours.

Maybe someone in the post office took it off.'

'You won't find out tonight,' said Neil. 'They shut five minutes ago.'

'Typical,' said Julie, and glared at the display of padded envelopes and hearts in the window. *Send love to someone this Valentine's Day*, a sign proclaimed.

'Well, I'll leave you to your deductions, Miss Marple,' said Neil. 'I popped into the village for carrots. Beef stew tonight.' He half-lifted a shopping bag.

'Oh, very nice,' Julie said, automatically. She had gone back to cooking at night now, having exhausted the cafeteria's limited options, but her meals tended to be simple and she never cooked any of Jason's favourites.

'See you around,' said Neil, and strode off. Julie wondered whether she should have offered him a lift. Then again, he probably felt like a walk after a day at his desk. *Besides*, she thought sourly, *he thinks the postbox topper going missing is funny. Miss Marple, indeed. He'll be laughing on the other side of his face when I catch the person who did it.*

4

At the next meeting of Hooked on Yarn, everyone seemed subdued. People said hello and exchanged pleasantries, but no one took out their work. They eyed each other, waiting.

'So, Julie, anything to feed back?' said Miriam. Her voice was casual yet kind, as if enquiring how a minor operation had gone. Removing an ingrown toenail, for instance.

'I've made enquiries,' said Julie. 'No one's reported anything to the parish council, and the police were no help.'

Tegan snorted and began to unpack the uterus she had been working on, which didn't want to come out of her bag.

'I also asked in the post office – several different people – but no one saw anything. Neither did any of the staff in that parade of shops. I've been in every shop in the village. The only thing I have managed to find out is that the postbox topper was still there at half past eleven that morning. One of the post-office workers said she saw it when she went to open the door for a customer, but when the postman came to collect from the box at noon, he asked where the topper had gone. So it disappeared between half eleven and twelve.'

'That's a narrow window,' said Miriam. 'Surely the village would have been fairly busy at that point. It was a nice day, wasn't it? For February.'

'The plot thickens,' said Lucy, and shrugged when everyone looked at her.

'I'll keep trying,' said Julie. 'At least I've narrowed it down.'

'You have,' said Miriam. 'Thanks for your hard work on this, Julie.' She sighed. 'But we have to accept that the postbox topper has probably gone for good.'

'I'll still keep trying,' said Julie. She felt her hands making fists and shoved them in her lap.

'So what do we do?' said Natalie. 'Do we make another topper, or what?'

'Let's vote on it and go with the majority,' said Miriam. 'That's the fairest thing to do. All those in favour of making another topper, raise your hands.'

Bernie's hand shot up, as did Natalie's. Lucy raised hers a few seconds later.

'I agree with you,' said Miriam. 'We should try again.' She put up her hand.

Vix looked round the room. 'I'm still annoyed about it,' she said, and raised her hand.

Tegan stared at her uterus, which was coming on nicely. 'It's not what I wanted to do in the first place,' she said. 'And I'm pretty sure that whoever pinched the first one will come back. But yeah, whatever.' She raised her hand.

Everyone looked at Julie. 'You might as well just say that you don't think I'll find the topper,' she said.

'I don't think Hercule Poirot could find this topper,' said Miriam. 'Or Inspector Morse, or anyone. There are no clues, and no leads. Anyway, we said majority vote. If you'd rather not make another topper, you can always work on something else. We won't mind.'

'Fine,' said Julie. 'As long as you know I'm against it.' She raised her hand to ear level.

'Right, motion carried.' Miriam was brisk again. 'Operation Replacement Postbox Topper is on. And this time I'll secure it so tightly that they'll need a chainsaw to get it off. That's a joke,' she added, looking around the group. 'Luckily, we still have enough yarn. Will we all do the same thing? Does anyone want to swap?'

'Could I swap with someone?' said Lucy. 'I've got a lot on at the moment and daffodils are quite fiddly.'

'I'll try, if you show me what to do,' said Julie. She regretted her words as as soon as she'd said them.

Lucy looked slightly sheepish. 'I followed a YouTube tutorial. I'll send it to the WhatsApp group. I can start you off, though.'

'Back to the killer ducks,' said Tegan, and stuffed her uterus in its bag.

***

On Friday, Julie tried to concentrate on her work, but her mind kept wandering to the postbox topper and who could possibly have taken it. Who would choose one of the busiest times of the day to steal something? And why hadn't anyone seen them?

With that in mind, she walked to the village at lunchtime on Saturday and loitered near the postbox. The village was teeming with people bringing parcels to post, getting meat from the butcher, popping into the delicatessen and heading for the coffee shop. Barely five seconds went by when someone didn't walk past the postbox. Admittedly, lots of them were talking to their companion or on their phones, but enough of them glanced curiously at Julie to convince her that anyone pinching the topper would have been spotted. Unless... Could the thief have created a psychological moment and made everyone look elsewhere? But how? Had they brought an accomplice?

Could the wind have blown it off? she thought.

Miriam said it wasn't very secure.

It would have to be a heck of a gust of wind. She checked the weather for that day. There had been a gentle breeze, at most. 'I bet Hercule Poirot never had to put up with this.'

A couple of people stared, then giggled, and Julie realised she had spoken out loud. She hurried away.

She felt peckish, but didn't want to brave the coffee shop. She had interrogated several shopkeepers, and so many people had given her odd glances that she feared they viewed her as an eccentric. Hopefully, a harmless one. *I'll stroll round the park, and go later.*

Once she got past the children laughing and screaming on the swings and slides, the park was quiet. Julie strolled along the path, musing. *If the Famous Five were investigating this, the postbox topper would probably be in a hollow tree. Or Uncle Quentin's study.*

Something rustled on her right, in what she thought of as the nature area, since it had bird boxes and a couple of feeders. A squirrel? Julie paused, listening. *Is it a sign?*

An image of bright wool protruding from a hole in a sturdy tree flashed into her mind. She left the path and tiptoed through the remains of leaves and stubby grass, listening.

Her foot sank into a leaf-covered hole. 'Ow!'

There was a great flapping of wings, and a large

black bird flew away.

A tall man in a waxed jacket and black wellies emerged from behind a tree. 'Thanks, I was watching that.' At the sound of his voice, Julie recognised Neil. His hair stuck out from under a khaki beanie. He frowned slightly. 'You all right, Julie? You haven't twisted your ankle, have you?'

'No. Um, sorry for disturbing you.' She registered the binoculars in his hand. 'You're a birdwatcher?'

'A birder, yes.' He raised his eyebrows. 'What are you smiling at?'

'Nothing,' said Julie, straightening her face. But he hadn't been exactly complimentary about her new hobby. 'I just didn't have you down as one of those people who stare at birds for hours.' Now that she thought of it, with his baggy jumpers, long legs and wild hair, Neil reminded her of a large, rather unkempt bird. The corner of her mouth crept up.

'Each to their own,' said Neil.

'You look as if you're dressed for an expedition.'

'It blends in with the background,' he said, unabashed.

Why aren't men ashamed of their hobbies, thought Julie. *Then again, why am I?* 'What sort of bird were you watching?' she asked.

'I was hoping for a woodpecker,' he said. 'I thought I saw one through the trees, but it didn't show itself. Although I did see a raven: the bird that just flew away. And all sorts of tits and sparrows and whatnot. Normally I go to the nature reserve on Saturdays but I don't have time today, so this will have to do.' He smiled. 'Anyway, enough about me and my funny habits. What brings you to the park on this chilly day? Stretching your legs?'

'Kind of,' said Julie. Then honesty got the better of her. 'I'm still trying to find the postbox topper. We're making another one, but… I suppose I want closure.'

'Oh.' She expected him to laugh or smirk, but he didn't. 'Good luck with that.' He looked at his watch. 'I'd better go, but if I spot anything or get any bright ideas, I'll let you know.' He raised his binoculars. 'Enjoy your walk.' Off he went, striding through the leaf-mould to the path and away.

Julie watched him go, her hand resting on the gnarled bark of a nearby tree. *It's kind of him to offer to help.* Her stomach rumbled. *It's time for me to go, too.*

She picked her way carefully back to the path, avoiding the now-obvious hole, and meandered towards the village. As she approached the gate, her eye caught a speck of yellow. Her heart leapt. Could it be…?

It was the bud of a miniature daffodil, bright against the stone post. *Oh well*, thought Julie. Nevertheless, that little yellow speck made her feel better. She wasn't sure why, but it did.

5

Julie felt considerably less well-disposed towards daffodils after several attempts to crochet one. The bit she'd done under Lucy's supervision in the library had been absolutely fine. That, however, was the easy part.

'How on earth did she make six of these?' she exclaimed, as she paused the YouTube video on her phone yet again and tried to rewind it to the right bit. She found what she wanted – or rather a few seconds before – but the ball of yarn wormed its way off her lap and rolled under the armchair. She tugged the end, which sent the ball further out of reach. She considered leaving it there, then considered the possibility of dust and spiders.

Julie paused the video, said a rude word quite loudly to relieve her feelings, put down her crochet and ferreted beneath the chair. The yarn came out with a bit of fluff attached, but nothing worse. She sighed, picked up the crochet and found the hook had detached itself so that she managed to undo the last three stitches. 'Aaargh!' She regarded the twisted mess, which reminded her of a miniature yellow alien, said another rude word, and went to make tea.

When Thursday evening came round, it found Julie in her armchair, crocheting and muttering. 'You can do this,' she told herself. 'You've made two of these ridiculous things and you've got a quarter of an hour to finish this one.' She glared at it. 'Watch out,' she told it, 'or you won't get your full complement of petals.'

The daffodil's trumpet regarded her insolently. 'Never again,' she said. 'Once I've made six of you, that's it. Daisies all the way next time.' She looked at her watch and continued to crochet.

As the minutes ticked away, her hook went faster and faster. Somehow, it acquired a will of its own, but in a good way. 'Come on,' she urged it. Then she realised she was talking to a crochet hook and remained silent until she completed the last stitch.

Carefully she fastened off and finished the daffodil, working the end of the yarn through the stitches. She dropped the flower on the coffee table. 'Yesss!' She threw her hands in the air. 'Free at last!' She glanced at the clock. 'And late!' She sprang up, stuffed the flowers and her materials in their bag, then ran to the little vestibule and shrugged on her coat.

As she was heading down the path, a door opened nearby. 'Er, Julie?' It was Neil's voice.

'I'm in a rush!' she cried. 'Can it wait?'

'Um, yes, I—'

'Great!' She gave him two thumbs up and hurried off.

***

Julie burst into the library, red-faced and panting. 'Sorry I'm late, I was finishing a daffodil.'

'I was about to message you,' said Vix, looking slightly cross. 'I wondered where you were.'

'Sorry,' said Julie. 'I got carried away. It's only five past, though.'

'How are you finding the daffodils?' asked Lucy.

'Honestly? Awful.'

Lucy laughed. 'They are, aren't they? I finished them out of a sense of duty. I must admit, I was glad when you volunteered to take them on.'

Julie grimaced. 'Thanks for nothing.' She saw an empty seat next to Tegan and hurried round the table. 'How is everyone?'

Bernie shrugged. 'Plodding on.' She looked at the postbox hat, which was starting to take shape. 'I meant to get more done, but— I haven't been in the mood.'

'I know what you mean,' said Tegan. 'Spite and bloodymindedness are keeping me going. I'm not letting the evil killer ducks beat me.'

Miriam laughed. 'That's the spirit.' Then her face grew serious. 'If people aren't feeling it, we don't have to make another topper. We can move on and do something else.'

'Absolutely not,' said Julie. 'I haven't sweated over these flaming daffodils to give up now.'

'I suppose there's no news of the topper,' said Bernie, wistfully.

'Sorry,' said Julie. 'I can't think of anything else to do. My neighbour said he'd keep an eye out – he's a birdwatcher so he's got binoculars.' Vix snorted. 'But I've mostly been swearing at these things in my spare time.' She took a daffodil out of her bag and shook it.

'Oh wow,' said Lucy, peering at it. 'That looks good. I kept going wrong with mine and having to unpick them.'

'They're so fiddly,' said Julie. 'Aren't you?' she asked the daffodil, and made it nod.

Tegan shuddered. 'That reminds me of a nightmare I had. Please don't make it talk.'

Julie gave her a sidelong glance and put the daffodil away.

She managed another half daffodil at the session. Every so often, she glanced around the table. Everyone was working steadily, but the mood was subdued. When they were working on the first topper there had been laughter and chat. Now there was quiet, slightly grim determination.

'How are we getting on?' Miriam asked, looking up from a half-finished crocus. 'Not that I'm hurrying you: I just want to get an idea of where we are.'

'Three and a half daffodils,' said Julie. 'And not a great deal of sanity.'

'Two killer ducks,' said Tegan.

'I'm dying to say a partridge in a pear tree,' said Natalie. 'Really, it's one and a half lambs.'

The list went round the table. Vix had produced an army of small yellow chicks. 'If anyone needs a hand, I've got capacity,' she said. 'Jules, are you managing OK?'

'I'm over halfway,' said Julie. 'I'm not going to be defeated by a flipping daffodil.'

'That's what we want to hear!' cried Vix, beaming. 'Stay *positive*, Jules.'

It's Julie, and you know that, Julie thought.

'So if we keep going at the same rate,' said Miriam, 'we could get the bits for the topper pretty much finished by the end of next week's session. Shall we aim for that?'

'Yeah, why not,' said Tegan.

Bernie interlaced her fingers and stretched her arms in front of her. 'I must admit, I'll be relieved to get it done. I found a fantastic pattern for a gorilla and I can't wait to make him.'

They parted at the door of the library with

goodbyes and Julie set off for home. It had gone chilly, more than she expected from mid-February. Then again, she hadn't been out at night for a long time. She zipped her coat right up to the top, stuck her hands in her pockets and walked faster.

She was about to head down her garden path when she remembered that Neil had wanted to speak to her earlier and went to knock on his door.

She was still waiting a minute later. *He can't have gone to bed*, she thought. *It's nine fifteen. And there are lights on, so presumably he's in.*

She saw movement behind the etched-glass panel in the door, followed by a dark shape looming closer, and it opened. 'Oh, hello,' said Neil. She was relieved to see he wasn't in his pyjamas, just another of his scruffy jumpers, teamed with black jeans. How many did he have? 'Sorry I took a while: I was working on something.'

'That's fine,' she said. 'You wanted to talk to me earlier?'

'Did I?' He looked puzzled. 'Oh yes, I wondered how you were getting on with the postbox top thingy.'

'The topper? Oh, we should finish it next week.'

'I meant investigating where the first one went. Have you made any progress?'

Julie sighed, puffing out a cloud of mist. 'To be honest, I've mostly been working on flowers for the new one.' She felt a pang of guilt. 'Thanks for asking, though.'

'It's just that I've had an idea.'

She stared at him. 'Have you?'

'I have!' He laughed, and she found herself smiling. 'It might be nothing, but I fell to wondering who on earth would bother to steal a postbox topper. No disrespect to the topper, you understand, but what else can you do with it? It's too big for a hat, the wrong shape for a tea cosy, and it's got weird stuff on it. Again, begging your pardon, all I could come up with was a rival knitter, or a group of them. Surely they're the only people who could possibly be interested.'

'I thought of something similar a while back,' said Julie, 'but I never followed it up. Someone in the group said they'd seen a postbox topper in Meadhurst. It's a faint possibility, but it's the first lead I've had. Thanks for reminding me, Neil.' She looked at her watch. 'I'll drive to Meadhurst now and do a recce. There can't be that many postboxes.'

'Now?' Neil's eyebrows shot up. 'Seriously?' He started laughing again. 'You could at least wait till it's light.'

He's got a point. 'Yeah, I suppose so,' said Julie. 'Fair enough, I'll head out early tomorrow and drive through Meadhurst on my way to work.'

'In that case,' said Neil, 'you'd better go and have your cocoa. Let me know how it goes.' He yawned.

'Sorry, too much staring at a screen. Probably time I knocked off.'

'You're still working?' It was Julie's turn to raise her eyebrows.

'Yup, got a deadline. That's the problem with working for yourself – the boss can be a right meanie.' He grinned.

'Well, I say you should take the rest of the day off, whatever your boss thinks.' She smiled back at him. 'Good night, Neil. And thanks.'

She walked down the path, then out by his garden gate, in by hers, and towards her own front door. *Silly, really. There ought to be a shortcut.* Neil was still in his doorway, so she waved and held up her keys. 'Don't worry, I can make it from here.'

'Night, Julie.' He went in.

Julie closed her door and leaned against it for a moment. Her heart was beating rapidly. *A lead*, she thought, *a proper lead! What if I find the postbox topper tomorrow?*

It's a slim chance, her more sensible self told her. *Does it matter, given that you're making another one anyway?*

That's not the point. I want to know. She went to put the kettle on, resolving to set her alarm for an hour earlier the next morning. 'The game is afoot,' she murmured.

6

Despite Julie's early alarm, she still woke half an hour before it went off. *Should I get up?*

Don't be silly, you won't be able to see anything. But she was wide awake and it was no use trying to doze. So she got up and made tea and toast, mulling over a plan of action. *What if I find the postbox topper?*

Bring it back, obviously.

What if someone sees me and thinks I'm stealing it? What do I do then?

Someone probably took a photo of it in the village.

But how do I prove it's the same one?

You can worry about that when you find it.

On impulse, she got her phone and looked in the WhatsApp group, but there were no photos of the postbox topper. *Why on earth didn't Miriam take one?*

With reluctance, she opened Facebook. She did

have a profile, but she barely used it. Some of the knitting group had mentioned craft projects they'd seen on Facebook, though, so maybe it was worth looking into. There was a village Facebook group: Neil had told her and Jason when they moved to Meadley. However, he'd said most of the posts were people moaning about speeding cars and young people on bikes. She found it – Meadley Village Chat – and scrolled through recent posts. Nothing. It was as if the postbox topper had never existed.

Julie closed her eyes and murmured 'It's real, I know it is.' She saw the time in the corner of her phone. *Honestly, stop woolgathering and get on with it.* She dressed warmly, in case she needed to leave the car somewhere and walk. Then she went to the kitchen drawer and took out a large pair of scissors which could cut through almost anything. 'Even if they've wired it on, I'll get it,' she muttered grimly. She pulled on a hat, got her keys and left, closing the door quietly in case Neil was up and doing. While it would have been useful to have another pair of eyes on the search, she could do without any wisecracks at her expense about following a trail of wool.

The roads were quiet. Julie usually left for work early anyway, to avoid the traffic, but lit by the first rays of a nondescript dawn, the road felt ghostly. At least it was warmer: a balmy four degrees, according to the car.

She drove along the winding country road, gripping the steering wheel tight and watching for the sign announcing that she was entering Meadhurst. 'There it is,' she whispered. 'I have to keep a lookout now.' And she slowed down.

Meadhurst was bigger than she remembered – not quite a town, but certainly a larger village than Meadley. She drove carefully, alert for a splash of red. Not that it would be bright red in this light, more a dark reddish-grey. *You mug. Why are you doing this? There must be someone else who could come here during the day.* She thought she saw something and her heart missed a beat. Then she realised it was a small red car and released her pent-up breath.

She came to what she remembered as the village centre, a sort of crossroads. *It does have a post office, doesn't it? If Meadley has one, surely this place does.*

There's only one way to find out. Julie turned left and drove slowly, glancing from side to side as if she was watching a long tennis rally at Wimbledon. Soon the shops, pubs and restaurants petered out, giving way to rows of houses and the occasional small apartment block. She found a safe place to turn round. *Maybe the next road.* At the crossroads, she took another left.

It was getting lighter. A postbox would be easier to spot. And she did spot one, but the postbox wore no topper, standing bald and proud outside the post office in the growing winter light. 'Damn,' said Julie, through gritted teeth. She kept going, looking for a side road, but there was a car behind her and it was a few minutes before she could safely turn round.

At the junction, she took the last arm of the crossroads. No postbox was there. *At least I tried*, she thought, and searched for somewhere to pull in.

As she turned into a pub car park, a horrible thought struck her. What if someone in Meadhurst *had* stolen the topper, but put it on a postbox in a side road? Or even hidden it? *They wouldn't do that. The whole point of a postbox topper is to have it where everyone can see it.* Nevertheless, the thought nagged her as she drove back to the crossroads.

Off to work, I suppose. She took the road for Meadborough. The car's clock said it was twenty past eight. She sighed. Normally, she was in work for eight thirty. But she always worked her hours, at least, and it wasn't as if she *had* to be in that early. It was just a habit. Nevertheless, she accelerated until she was driving at the speed limit. Then she glanced at the passenger seat. Her bag wasn't there. She huffed, and smacked the steering wheel lightly. *You idiot, Julie.*

What will I do for lunch? She remembered the ham salad sandwich she had made the night before, which was sitting in the fridge. And her purse was in the bag. Her phone was at home too, and sometimes work contacts rang or messaged her on it.

She growled, took the next side road, and found herself doing a seven-point turn.

Now, of course, everyone was going to work or dropping their kids at school. Every traffic light turned red as Julie approached it, but finally, thankfully, she reached her street and parked outside her house. She dashed in, grabbed her things, and pulled the door closed.

As she was locking it, Neil's front door opened. 'Hello there,' he called. 'Have you been topper hunting? I heard the squeal of wheels and smelt burning rubber.'

In spite of herself, Julie laughed. 'I have, but I didn't find one.' She advanced to the low fence which separated their gardens. 'I drove all round the main part of Meadhurst and I only found one postbox, never mind one with a hat on. I figured it wasn't worth searching the side streets because...'

'Because what?' said Neil, but Julie paid him no attention. Her gaze was fixed on something by Neil's shin. A jute shopping bag with a glimpse of soft, sickeningly familiar colours at the top: pale green, white and yellow.

'Wait right there.' She marched along her path then down Neil's, gathering momentum with every step. 'It was you, wasn't it?' She pointed an accusing finger, which to her annoyance trembled slightly. 'You, all the time. Why, Neil? What have I ever done to you?

Why can't I have hobbies? Don't I deserve them? Aren't I *allowed* to enjoy myself? You've been laughing behind my back, haven't you? Asking me about the topper and sending me on a wild-goose chase!'

Neil took a step back. 'I'm not sure what you—'

'It's right there!' If she could have stabbed him with her finger, she would have. 'You haven't even bothered to hide it. I bet you've enjoyed standing at the door chatting with me, knowing it's two feet away.'

Neil's gaze followed the direction of her finger. Slowly, he picked up the bag, drew out a ball of white wool and dropped it on the floor. Then a yellow one, then a green. His face was expressionless.

Julie stared at them, then him. 'What—'

'I was in the charity bookshop in Meadhurst – checking out a book about birds, surprisingly enough – and they had wool in. It looked like the right colours for your new postbox topper, so I bought some. When I told the manager what it was for, she gave me a discount: turns out she lives in Meadley. I meant to give it to you – that's why it's by the door – but work's been busy and I forgot.' He swiped the balls of wool from the floor, dropped them in the bag and thrust it at her. 'You might as well take it; I've no use for it. Now, if you'll excuse me.' He pulled the door to smartly, not looking at her.

Julie stood nonplussed, the bag of wool in her arms. Slowly, she bent and opened the flap of the letterbox. 'Neil, I'm sorry.' Her voice was shaking. *For heaven's sake.* 'I have to go to work. I'm late already.'

Silence.

'I really am sorry, but it did look like…' She let the letterbox flap fall and trailed down the path to her car.

She arrived at work just after nine, but all the parking spaces near the building were taken. It took her ten minutes to find a parking space and reach her office, where she found her boss perched on her desk, arms folded. 'Why are you so late, Julie?'

She consulted her watch. 'I know I'm later than usual, Greg, but the flexitime policy says—'

'You're always in for eight thirty. Not that it matters normally, but I've had complaints.'

She froze. 'A complaint?'

'Not *a* complaint. Complaint*sss*.' He actually hissed at her. 'Yes. That report you were meant to go through. When I sent it out yesterday afternoon, I didn't expect to come in this morning to a load of emails from our clients pointing out multiple errors.'

'What kind of errors?'

'The point is, Julie, you're meant to make sure reports are error free *before* I send them.'

'I made lots of corrections,' she said, in a daze.

'Not enough. I don't want jokey little emails from my clients saying *Not up to your usual high standard* or *Someone's having an off day*. From what I understand, you've had more than one off day lately. I heard on the grapevine that you've joined some sort of ladies' knitting circle and you've been getting excited over a stupid *postbox* hat. What you do in your own time is your business, but when it starts affecting your work, you'd better think on. Do I make myself clear?'

'Yes.' It was almost a whisper.

He leaned forward. 'What was that?'

'Yes, Greg. Sorry, Greg.' She swallowed. 'I won't let it happen again.'

'Make sure you don't.' The desk creaked as he rose. 'There won't be a formal sanction this time, but if it happens again…' He gave her a contemptuous look and walked out.

On autopilot, Julie hung up her things, sat down and switched on her computer. She stared at the company logo on her screen, then got up, closed the door and put her face in her hands, hoping nobody could hear her crying.

7

Eventually, Julie made herself a strong cup of tea and dared to face her email. She'd already checked her phone, which had been on silent, and seen various messages from Greg.

8:40: *Where are you? I want a word*

8:52: *Are you all right? I checked your work calendar and you ought to be in by now*

8:59: *Please report to me as soon as you get in*

9:05: *Has something happened? I rang but the phone went to voicemail. I left a message. Ring me asap*

Julie listened to the message. *Hi, Julie, it's Greg. Your boss. Wondering where you are. We need to talk. Hope you're OK, I'm a bit worried. Right, yes, bye.*

She bit her lip and deleted it. *What a morning. I've*

managed to annoy my boss, make a complete fool of myself and wrongly accuse Neil. He'll probably never speak to me again. She remembered his face as he had dropped the wool on the floor, and sighed. *He did something nice for me and I thought the worst of him.*

At the top of her email inbox was a message headed *MANDATORY FIRE TRAINING – OVERDUE*. Apparently, she ought to have completed the online training module by the previous Friday. 'Silly me,' murmured Julie. She wasn't in the mood for clicking her way through a series of questions she could have answered in her sleep. But a quiz she could do in her sleep was probably the safest option on a day like today. The worst that could happen was that she had to redo the module. She glanced through the rest of her email in case there was anything urgent, then clicked the link.

Q1: What sort of fire extinguisher should you use in the event of an electrical fire?
A: foam
B: water
C: carbon dioxide

Julie clicked C and pressed *Submit*.

Correct! Well done! Are you ready for the next question?

Julie huffed and selected *Yes*.

She clicked her way through the questions and achieved a score of 85%, which the system told her was a pass. *There's room for improvement though, Julie. Would you like to retake the test?*

Julie rolled her eyes and clicked the button which said *No, thanks*.

That done, and a certificate printed for her records, she sipped her cooling tea and closed her eyes. *I should go and apologise properly to Greg. He was actually worried about me.*

She finished her drink and stood up just as someone knocked on the door. 'With you in a minute,' she said, and inspected herself in the pocket mirror she kept in her bag. She was still a bit red around the eyes, but otherwise appeared pretty much as normal. 'Come in!'

Greg put his head round the door, looking sheepish. 'I came to say sorry.'

'Oh.' She managed a smile. 'I was about to come and do the same thing.'

'Ah. Mind if I sit down?' He eyed the chair in front of her desk.

'Of course you can.' She resumed her seat behind the desk. This was odd. Usually she went to see Greg. Now, it almost felt as if she was the boss. What a thought.

'I didn't mean to have a go at you earlier,' he said.

'I hadn't even noticed the errors in the report until I started getting emails pointing them out. A few typos, that was all.'

Julie shrugged. 'I'm sorry I missed them. As I said, I'll do my best to make sure it doesn't happen again. If in future I think I'll be in much past eight thirty, I'll send a message. I'm sorry you were worried, Greg. And I'll make sure my phone isn't on silent.'

'Thanks.' Greg shifted in his seat. 'It was what your friend said that wound me up. And worried me.'

'My friend? Do you mean Vix?'

'Very enthusiastic, tall and a bit chunky, works in sales. Don't tell her about the chunky bit.'

'That would be her.' Curiosity got the better of Julie. 'What did she say?'

'I didn't go seeking her out, you understand. I saw her in the corridor this morning and asked if she knew where you were. She launched into this big spiel about how she'd invited you to her knitting group because you were so sad and lonely and you were trying to track down a – a missing postbox topper?' He sounded as if he was attempting to speak a foreign language he'd never studied. 'She said you'd become obsessed with it and you didn't have anything else to live for.' He huffed out a breath. 'That's what worried me. I thought you might have—'

'*Me?*' Julie stared at him. 'Things aren't that bad.

OK, I'm not partying every night, but—'

'I hope I haven't spoken out of turn,' said Greg. 'I'm sure she means well.'

'I daresay she thinks she does,' Julie said grimly. She clenched her hands into fists, realised what she was doing, and clasped them instead.

Greg scrutinised her with a frown. 'You still look pale,' he said. 'I'm not sure you should be in work today.'

'I'm fine. I've done my fire training and everything.'

He peered at the certificate. '85%? That's definitely a sign you're not right.'

'It's still a pass,' Julie countered. 'It'll do.'

It was his turn to stare at her. 'You never think like that. You *never* let anything go. That's probably what your friend means about this postbox business. I bet you've been spending every hour outside work looking for the damn thing, whatever it is. I'm used to you picking through everything, holding us to account and keeping us on target. You're a machine.'

She raised her eyebrows. 'Am I? A machine?'

'I didn't mean it like that. I meant you're great at it, and I value that immensely. It's— This line of work is very competitive. We need to be the best just to survive, and you're a big part of that. Even tiny little errors make a difference.' Greg ran a hand through his short, greying hair, and Julie suddenly realised that he seemed a fair bit older than he had when she joined the company three years before. 'You should head home. You look terrible.'

'Thanks,' said Julie, with a wry smile.

'Can someone come and fetch you? I'm not sure you should be driving. Or maybe your friend could—'

'I'm fine to drive,' Julie said firmly.

Greg looked dubious. 'I'd take you, but I'm in a meeting in ten minutes.' His face cleared. 'I'll get reception to ring a taxi for you. Take a, what is it, a mental health day. It's Friday anyway, nothing ever happens on a Friday. Your car will be fine in the car park.'

'Yes, but—' For a second, Julie thought of phoning Neil. She had his number in her phone, for emergencies. *That ship has sailed,* she thought sadly. 'OK.'

'Great.' Greg stood up and rolled his shoulders. 'It'll do you the world of good.'

'Maybe you're right.' Julie logged off her computer and packed her bag. *At least my lunch had a nice trip in. I can fetch the car later, when Greg is taking his usual Friday long lunch.*

***

Julie spent the taxi ride home analysing various bits of the conversation she had had with Greg. 'Machine, indeed,' she muttered.

'Sorry, love?' said the taxi driver.

'Nothing, sorry.' *And as for Vix...* She scowled. *Am I being too hard on her? Am I obsessed? I suppose I am lonely, but I'm not sad. Not all the time, anyway. And I'm a lot less sad than I was. I have Vix to thank for that. If she hadn't invited me to the group—*

None of this would have happened, said a precise voice in her head.

I wouldn't have enjoyed myself spending time with the group and learning a new skill, Julie insisted. *And I'm grateful. Vix isn't perfect, but she means well. You can't expect people to be perfect.* Neil flashed into her mind, with his long hair, his dry humour, his scruffy jumpers and his silly birdwatching clothes. Not that they were silly, in context. *I'm not perfect, far from it. Maybe I should accept that.*

'What number is it, love?' asked the driver.

'Thirty-two.'

The taxi slowed to a stop. 'Very nice,' the driver said, approvingly. 'Got your things?'

'I think so.' Julie checked her bag. Then she considered the question more broadly. *You have a home, a job, friends, a hobby...* She closed her eyes for a moment and saw Neil, smiling at her. *You have everything you need, if you'd only see it.*

She thanked the driver and got out, then steeled herself and opened Neil's gate.

He might be out, she thought, as she walked down the path.

She knocked and waited. *He might be busy working. He said he had a deadline.*

Or he might be ignoring you.

She waited another minute, then knocked again, harder.

'Scuse me, love.' The taxi driver was leaning out of his window. 'Should I hang on? It's just that I've got another job to go to.'

'Oh no, please go. I live in the house next door. I don't think he's in, anyway.' She jerked her thumb at the door and it opened. Neil stood in the doorway, his hair wet and his T-shirt on inside out. Julie blinked, twice.

'I was in the shower,' he explained. 'What's happened? Why have you come home? You never do that during the day. You haven't—'

'I'll let you two get on,' said the driver, grinning. He closed his window and moved off slowly.

Julie turned to Neil. 'I'm so sorry about earlier. I can explain.' Water was dripping onto the shoulders of his T-shirt, which clung to him. She had a sudden vision of him in the shower that made her take a step back. 'I'm sorry I disturbed you. I should go.'

'You look as if you need a cup of tea,' said Neil. He opened the door wider and stood aside, and she walked into the house.

8

'As I said, I'm really sorry, and I should have thought before jumping in and accusing you of—'

Neil held up a hand. 'You can stop apologising, Julie. I get it: you made a mistake and you're sorry. I accept your apology. And I can see why you jumped to conclusions.'

'The wrong concl—'

He laughed. 'Have you finished that tea yet?'

Julie glanced at the inch or so of tea in her mug. 'Almost.' She drained it. 'I'm sorry. You must have work to do, and here I am in your sitting room unburdening myself.' Neil's sitting room was surprisingly nice, with a large squashy sofa, a colourful rug on the wooden floor, and modern art prints on the cream walls. She had already checked the bookcase for mystery novels. *Nobody's perfect.*

Neil smiled. 'As it happens, I don't have any work

to do. Not that won't wait. The deadline for the thing I was working on is at noon today, but I got it in yesterday evening. I hate leaving things till the last minute.'

'Do you? I do too.' She hadn't seen Neil as particularly organised. It was probably the hair and the jumpers.

'I may look like a scruffy herbert,' said Neil, 'but I'm actually quite business-minded. Anyway, what I was going to say, before we went off on a tangent, was that I'm heading to the nature reserve for a walk and a bit of birdwatching. I wondered if you wanted to come.'

'Me?'

He laughed. 'Yes, you. I mean, if you have other things to be getting on with—'

'No, not at all.' She put her mug on the coffee table. 'It's just that I can identify a blackbird and that's about it.'

'Oh dear,' said Neil. 'The nature reserve won't let you in if you fail the bird test.'

'The bird te— Oh.' She giggled, which surprised her. 'Are you sure you don't mind?'

His eyebrows drew together for a moment. 'I wouldn't have invited you if I minded, would I?' He eyed her work shoes. 'Although maybe you should change your shoes. There could be puddles.'

'OK.' Julie stood up. 'I'll give you a knock in five

minutes.'

At home, she put her lunch in the fridge and ran upstairs. The jumper she had on was fine, but the knee-length skirt would be ridiculous in a nature reserve. She changed into jeans, brushed her hair, then went to the bathroom and washed her face. Would it be overkill to put on make-up? She checked her watch. *It won't matter if I'm a minute late*, she thought, and reached for her mascara.

Neil gave her trainers an approving look. 'Right, let's go.' He'd put on similar clothes to the gear he'd worn in the park, but somehow it didn't seem silly now. He picked up a satchel. 'Where's your car, by the way? You came home in a taxi.'

'At work,' said Julie. 'My boss didn't want me to drive.' The minute she said it, she regretted the words. *He'll think I'm odd.*

'Don't see why,' said Neil. 'I can take you to fetch it later. So long as you promise not to ram me.'

'You'd better show me some good birds, then,' said Julie, and grinned.

Neil's car was small, and she was surprised when it moved without warning. 'Oh, it's electric,' she said.

'Yeah. Silent and sneaky.'

'I hadn't noticed.' There was so much she hadn't noticed, for such a long time.

The nature reserve was closer than Julie had realised. The sun had come out, and its rays did their best to get through the bare branches of the trees. 'We can do a loop of the hides,' said Neil. 'That way, hopefully you'll spot a variety of birds. Assuming they play ball.'

The first hide had posters on the walls with pictures of birds that frequented the nature reserve. Unfortunately, they were elsewhere that day. In the absence of birds, Neil taught Julie how to use the binoculars and she focused on different things: the bird feeder, a clump of snowdrops in a dell, another bird hide on the other side of the clearing. In the slit which served as a window she could see another birder in an army jacket, hiding behind a camera with a huge lens. 'The paparazzi are out,' she said, and handed Neil the binoculars.

He panned around the landscape. 'Oh yes. That'll be Frank the Flash.' He lowered the binoculars. 'You're pretty good with these.'

Julie was about to say that she'd seen Frank by chance, then checked herself. 'Thanks. I had a good teacher.'

'Flattery will get you everywhere,' said Neil. 'Let's try another hide. The birds must be somewhere. Not the one Frank's in, though: he'll shush you if you talk.'

They left the hide and strolled. Julie had expected Neil to be the sort of man who strode away and left you to catch up, but he walked as if there was plenty of time. 'What is it you do?' she asked. 'I know you work from home, and that you work for yourself.'

'I'm an environmental consultant,' said Neil. 'Building firms come to me when they're planning a new housing estate or retail park and I advise them on what to do to maintain local biodiversity.'

'Oh, right.'

'I used to work in an office, at a collar-and-tie sort of job, but I decided to go it alone after my wife ran off with her boss.'

Julie's eyes widened. 'I'm so sorry. I didn't mean to poke my nose in.'

'You didn't, I told you. It was five years ago: I'm over it now. We had to sell the house, of course, so I chose to find somewhere smaller than the fancy place we'd been struggling to pay for and do what I wanted for a change.'

'I don't blame you.' She blinked. She had always assumed Neil was a confirmed bachelor – in other words, grumpy and set in his ways. How had they never had a conversation like this before, in three years of living next door to each other? *You know why. You were too busy dealing with your own pain. Or not.*

'How about you?' he asked. 'What made you move to Meadley?'

'It was my – it was Jason's idea and I went along with it. It was meant to be a step towards retirement.

Not that I don't like Meadley: it's very nice. But it's difficult to leave the place and the people you know.'

'It is. I didn't realise until after we broke up how much stuff we did as a couple, and how much of a spare part I felt as a single man. Anyway, enough reminiscing. Let's try this hide.'

The second hide was more basic, and without posters. They opened the wooden flaps that covered the window slots and got comfortable on the high wooden bench. 'Here.' Neil passed Julie the binoculars. 'You have first go and tell me what you see.'

'OK.' Julie took the binoculars, hung the strap round her neck, and focused. 'Bird on the lake, black with a white bit on its head. Don't know what that is.'

'That's a coot,' said Neil. 'Any ducks?'

'No ducks,' said Julie, 'not even killer ones.' She could feel Neil staring at her. 'Sorry, that's a crochet joke.'

'You're a wild bunch when you get together, you lot.'

'Like you wouldn't believe.' She panned up. 'Oh, there's a bird on a feeder… Is it a blue tit?' She described it.

'That sounds about right.'

'It's flown off.' Julie scanned the landscape for anything else of interest. 'A black bird flew towards the trees. Not a blackbird, a black bird, and it's…

Wait.' She turned the focusing wheel. 'It can't be.'

'A black bird might be a crow or a raven,' said Neil. 'Then again, it might just be a big blackbird.'

Julie continued to stare through the binoculars. 'Near the top of a tree, there's something green and blue with little bits of white and yellow.' She fought to keep her voice steady. 'Could you have a look, please? To make sure I'm not hallucinating.' She gripped the binoculars tightly, ducked out of the strap and gave them to Neil.

'Let's see.' She watched his profile as he gazed through the binoculars. His eyes crinkled at the corners as he focused. He said nothing for a few seconds, then lowered the binoculars. 'Yup,' he said, 'that's a pair of ravens. I think I said I'd seen one the other day, in the park. They've pinched your postbox topper for their nest.'

Julie stared at him, then started laughing.

'You're taking it pretty well,' said Neil, smiling.

'I'm not climbing up there for it!' She grinned at him. 'At least they're making good use of it. And it's nice that nobody stole it. No human, anyway.'

'This is true,' said Neil.

'Wait till I tell the group,' she said. 'They won't believe it. It's a shame we can't get a photo. I don't think my phone can manage it.'

'I doubt mine can, but I know the man to ask. Come on, let's find Frank.' Neil put the caps on his binoculars and stood up.

'Why not,' said Julie. She followed him out of the hide, chuckling to herself.

9

'It gives me great pleasure to unveil the new Meadley village postbox topper.' The mayor pulled on the ribbon round the cloth-draped postbox and it fell to the ground. The cloth, however, didn't move.

Miriam and Bernie, who were standing nearby, lifted the fabric and revealed the topper.

'Ooo,' breathed the actually quite large crowd.

Tim from the paper (as Miriam had referred to him when persuading Julie that the tale of the postbox topper would make a brilliant story for the *Meadborough and District Times*) nudged the photographer, who snapped a few pictures. 'Now one with the knitting group,' Tim said. 'Come on, ladies. Let's have you gathered round the postbox.'

'Go on then,' said Neil, nudging Julie.

'Do I have to? I always look uncomfortable in photos, like I want to be somewhere else.'

'The paper wouldn't be here if it wasn't for you,' said Neil. 'You've only got yourself to blame.'

'All right,' said Julie. She stuck a smile on her face and walked forward.

'That's it, Julie, stand next to the postbox,' said Tim. 'Maybe point to the ravens.'

Tegan had been delighted when Julie told them the full story of the postbox topper at the next meeting. 'I love ravens!' she cried. 'They're so smart and black and Gothic, with all that croaking and nevermore. Right, I'm gonna make two ravens to go on the new topper.'

'Won't that look odd?' said Vix. 'They're not exactly springlike.'

'They'll be the only wildlife on the postbox topper that's actually been anywhere near it,' Tegan pointed out. 'Anyway, it's good practice for Halloween.' She fetched a ball of black yarn, plonked it on the table and pulled out her crochet hook with a determined air.

Miriam sighed. 'Don't make them too Gothic, Tegan.'

'Don't worry, they'll be cute.'

Julie, smiling for the camera, gave the ravens a sidelong glance. They weren't cute, exactly, but the nest between them, filled with knitted eggs, definitely softened the effect.

'Lovely,' called Tim. 'Julie, is your friend here? The chap who was with you when you found the postbox topper?'

Julie grinned. 'Oh yes.' She beckoned Neil. 'Come on, Neil, time for your moment of glory.'

'Not again,' said Neil, but she had already noted that the jumper he was wearing was one of his less baggy ones and he had definitely brushed his hair that morning.

'One on each side, George?' Tim asked the photographer.

'Let's have you standing together,' said the photographer, regarding them critically. 'Neil, can you stand behind Julie and maybe put a hand on her arm?'

Julie tried not to jump as Neil's hand touched her elbow. Even through the layers of coat and jumper, she felt it. She wouldn't have been surprised if her arm had glowed.

'Lovely. Say postbox topper.'

'Postbox topper!' they chorused, trying not to laugh.

'I defy the smartest of ravens to get that off,' said Miriam, once the photographer had finished. She tapped the wire which secured the topper round the postbox. 'That was excellent publicity for the group. Thanks to Julie.'

'Not to mention my new side hustle,' said Tegan. 'I've got five orders for life-size killer ducks, and two people have already enquired about ravens.'

'What are you calling your business again?' said

Bernie.

'Feminist Death Knits,' said Tegan.

'Ah,' said Bernie, 'of course. Well, I'd better make tracks. My grandson's coming for a sleepover and I need to hide everything breakable.'

'Yeah, bye,' muttered Vix, and hurried away.

'What's up with her?' asked Tegan, gazing at Vix's retreating back.

'It's a long story,' said Julie.

Vix had knocked on Julie's office door at ten to five the day before. 'Was it you who set Human Resources on me?' she asked, without preamble.

'No,' said Julie. 'I haven't said anything about you to anyone.' She wondered what on earth Greg had said.

'Huh,' said Vix. 'I was just trying to help, but *some* people don't appreciate it. I could do without being given a lecture on gossip and oversharing in the workplace and sent on team dynamics training.'

'I'm sorry about that,' said Julie, 'but I honestly haven't spoken to HR.'

Vix sniffed. 'Well, someone did, Jules. Enjoy your weekend.'

'It's Julie. Not Jules.'

Vix peeled herself off the doorframe, stepped out of Julie's office and shut the door, quite loudly.

'Hope you enjoy your weekend too,' called Julie, but there was no reply.

She was roused from her memory by Miriam clapping her hands. 'While you're still here – most of you – we'll be talking new projects at the group on Thursday. Julie has exciting news to share.'

Natalie's eyes widened. 'You can't tease us like that!'

'Just did,' said Miriam, grinning. 'Now, I've got kids to take swimming and I believe you have too, Natalie.'

Natalie checked her watch. 'Oh heck. Bye, everyone!' And she hurried off, Miriam's bombshell entirely forgotten.

'So what's the big news?' Neil asked, as they strolled towards home. 'I promise not to spill the beans.'

'It's really not that big,' said Julie.

'Knowing you, that probably means it's massive.'

She laughed 'It isn't. You'll probably think it's ridiculous.'

He stuck his hands in his pockets. 'Try me.'

'All right, I'm reducing my hours at work.'

'Wow, that is big. How come?'

'I thought about what you said, that I'm never at home during the day. You're right. I don't need to work full-time hours, and there are lots of other things I'd like to do with my time.'

Neil raised his eyebrows. 'Such as?'

'I've never been a hobby sort of person. I've

always been very into my work. I mostly went along with what Jason wanted to do. Maybe it's time to find out what *I* want to do. Plus an opportunity has come up.'

'Tell me more.'

'A company called Occasion Knits contacted me. They do commissions for events and launches and art installations. I think they got the wrong end of the stick, to be honest. They read the first article in the paper, which said I was a project manager, and they put that and the postbox topper together.'

'Sensible people, if you ask me.'

'Anyway, they asked if I'd do some ad hoc work with them on their bigger projects, managing the knitters and the products and so on. I tried to pass them on to Miriam, but she wasn't having any of it. Other villages have approached us about making postbox toppers for them, or talking to their knitting groups about where to begin. And I've offered to do spreadsheets for Tegan to help her keep on top of Feminist Death Knits. I'm even getting used to the name.' She smiled. 'Plus I want more time to crochet myself. So I'm moving to four days a week on a trial basis. My boss wasn't happy, but I told him it would improve my work-life balance.'

Neil pondered this as they walked. 'I reckon you'll be busier than before.'

'It's possible. Hopefully, in a good way. I decided

it was time for something new.'

'A fresh start?'

'Something like that.' They fell silent.

Julie stole a glance at Neil. It was nice to walk next to someone and feel as if you sort of belonged there. She would always love Jason, and always miss him, but it was time to move on. It had been a long, long winter, but now it felt as if spring was coming.

'I've been learning about ravens,' she said.

'Oh yes?' They were almost at the red telephone box which served as the local book swap. Neil fell in behind her, then caught her up once they had passed it.

'I knew about the ravens at the Tower of London, obviously, but I didn't know how smart they are. No wonder they managed to steal the postbox topper. Perhaps one created a psychological moment in the village which allowed the other one to steal the topper.'

Neil stared at her. 'Do you really think so? A postbox topper heist?'

'Who knows? It's a good story.'

'It is.'

They were almost home, and the pace had slowed somewhat. 'I read that they mate for life,' said Julie, casually. 'That's rather nice, if it's true.'

'I suppose it is,' said Neil. 'Although ravens are probably less complicated than humans.'

'Yes. Life's probably easier for ravens in that respect.'

The corner of Neil's mouth quirked up. 'I imagine so.'

'I'm glad I'm not a raven, though.' She moved a little closer, but kept walking.

'Me too. I'm not keen on heights, for one thing. And there are other reasons.' Neil's hand brushed hers.

Julie hesitated a moment, then touched Neil's hand. Gently, his fingers closed around hers. 'Could you fit a cup of tea into your busy schedule?' he asked.

She smiled up at him. 'I'd be delighted.'

Six months later...

Julie now works three days a week. One of her first projects took place in her front garden: removing a fence panel and creating a path between her house and Neil's. She and her team have created and delivered a zoo's-worth of woollen animals, a giant cobweb installation with matching spider, and a life-size knitted three-piece suite. Julie can recognise twenty-five different birds, and in her spare time she is making Neil a jumper that fits for Christmas.

Tegan's Feminist Death Knits are sold online and in gift shops throughout Meadborough and she has taken on another knitter. Julie has had to expand her original spreadsheets. The most popular items are ravens (particularly the deluxe edition with red eyes that light up), but Tegan still sells the occasional uterus. She is working on a design for a Halloween postbox topper.

Following the unveiling of the postbox topper, Hooked on Yarn acquired so many new members that Miriam had to find a larger venue. She coordinates several knitting groups in Meadborough and is talking about starting a nationwide knitting and crocheting network. She has also negotiated a discount on bulk yarn deliveries with a major supplier.

Vix still comes to the group occasionally, but she tends to sit with the new people. She says she is taking them under her wing.

Bernie completed her gorilla, which was immediately claimed by her grandson. He takes Bananas everywhere with him, and Bananas always receives compliments.

Lucy decided to make some easy-to-follow crochet videos, and now has her own YouTube channel.

The next time Jake had a food tantrum, Natalie offered him a plate of crocheted fish fingers, chips, peas and sweetcorn instead. He was so surprised that he shut up and ate his meal.

Greg suggested HR bring in duvet days and co-delivers a session on staff burnout to new managers. He's considering cutting his hours to four days a week.

Neil asked Julie to teach him how to knit. He makes squares in front of the TV and drops them off at the nature reserve for birds to line their nests with. He also writes a monthly column about birdwatching for the local paper. He's thinking of suggesting a birding trip to the Scottish Highlands next spring, but he's not sure Julie will be able to fit it in.

The Corner Shop

1

Saffron was about to hit the snooze button again when she registered that the bedroom was light. Far too light for the time of day it ought to be. 'Damn,' she whispered, rolled out of bed and headed straight for the en suite. No time to wash her hair: dry shampoo would have to do.

I shouldn't have waited up, she thought, as she removed a layer of skin with a body mitt. *Flaming Americans. Flaming Americans who can't make decisions.* She turned off the water, grabbed a towel, wrapped herself in it and glanced in the mirror.

God, you look tired. She opened the bathroom cabinet and gazed wistfully at the Crème de la Mer and Touche Éclat. *Only for special occasions*, she said firmly to herself, as she reached for the supermarket dupe moisturiser that was really quite good. And worlds cheaper.

Having assumed a protective layer, and added both lift and volume to her hair (which should have been highlighted two months ago to stay on schedule), she put on her white waffle bathrobe and went to the bedroom door. 'Aurora! Chad! Breakfast time!' Then she went downstairs, made herself a strong black coffee, took her vitamins and put out breakfast bowls and glasses of milk.

Chad was down first, a small scruffy thunderbolt yawning fit to bust. He picked up the cornflake packet and filled his bowl to the top.

'Are you going to eat all that?'

'Yeah.' He reached for the milk, then paused. 'Are these different cornflakes? They're the wrong colour.'

'No,' said Saffron. 'Same box, see. Maybe they changed the recipe. They do that sometimes.'

'Oh.' He flooded the bowl with milk.

'Any sign of your sister?'

He turned and yelled 'Roar!'

Saffron winced. 'There's no need to shout and your sister's name is Aurora.'

He grinned. 'Everyone calls her Roar. Even the headteacher.'

Saffron just resisted putting her head in her hands. *So much for picking names that couldn't be shortened.* Instead, she went to the foot of the stairs. 'Aurora! You'll be late for school if you're not careful.'

On the little table in the hall were three letters which had arrived yesterday. They were unopened. She had left them because the kids were with her, and she needed a positive mindset for the call with New York, and, well, because. Two bills, one with red writing on the envelope, which she had moved to the bottom. The other was a letter from her ex-husband's solicitors. 'More good news, no doubt,' she muttered, and ripped it open.

Dear Ms Montgomery,

We are writing to remind you that from the first of July, your maintenance payments will reduce. This is due to a change in the financial circumstances of your former husband. As we wrote previously, this will represent a reduction of £825 in your monthly payments.

If the situation changes, we will of course keep you informed. Please contact us if there is anything you wish to discuss.

Perhaps it was the coffee, but Saffron's muscles tensed and her heart banged in her chest. She forced herself to take deep slow breaths and stuffed the letter in her bathrobe pocket. 'Aurora!' she yelled. 'Get up *now!*'

'I am up,' Aurora protested. 'I'm doing my sun salutation.'

'Never mind that, you should be eating your breakfast.'

Eventually, both children were breakfasted and in their school uniforms – Aurora's skirt was well above her knees, suggesting yet another growth spurt – and Saffron was suitably armoured in skinny jeans, high-heeled ankle boots and a Breton top. 'We'll have to drive,' she said. 'Shoes on.'

Chad shoved his feet in his shoes without untying the laces. 'Oh Chad, you'll ruin them.'

'No I won't,' said Chad. 'Everyone does it.'

'That doesn't mean you have to. Come *on*, Aurora.'

Aurora was making a face at her left foot, encased in its regulation T-bar shoe. 'It doesn't fit.'

A chill gripped Saffron. 'Don't buckle it so tight.'

'I'm *not*. I can hardly get my foot in. I definitely can't wiggle my toes like the shoe lady says.'

Saffron nearly expressed a very forthright opinion of the shoe lady. Instead, she examined the thickness of Aurora's ankle socks, which was no help at all. 'We've got three options. Make do as you are, try them without socks, or wear your trainers.'

'Trainers!' cried Aurora, and shot towards the shoe rack like a streak of lightning.

***

Saffron was fuming when she finally got the 4x4 off the drive. *Bad things always come in threes. How many is that?* Two bills, a solicitor's letter, new shoes, and no doubt grumbles from school about the trainers. That made five, which meant something else was in store for her.

Positive thoughts. Deep breaths.

A driver drove out of the side road without looking and she leaned on her horn.

'This is what happens when you mess around before school,' she said, into the rear-view mirror. 'We have to be on the road with idiots and risk getting killed.'

'I can't help my feet growing,' Aurora said sadly. 'What are you doing today, Mummy?'

Working out how I can possibly afford new school shoes which will probably be too small by September, thought Saffron. 'I have calls with a couple of clients and I'll be working on a business expansion plan.' *If it's possible to expand a business which is practically dead on its feet in these interesting times.* 'Do you know what you'll be doing?'

'We're starting our new topic,' said Aurora. 'It's called Where We Live.'

'Oh, that sounds nice. What about you, Chad?'

'Dunno. Stuff.'

'Of course.' She turned into Beech Lane and passed the book swap, which was currently wearing a crocheted topper consisting of a large, striped worm wearing spectacles and reading a book. She rolled her eyes. *What some people find time to do.*

As they approached the school, both sides of the road were lined with cars.

'We've got to turn round,' said Chad. 'We can't park here.'

'No time,' said Saffron. She kept going, past the turning circle...

'Mummy!' cried Aurora.

'There's a space,' said Saffron, pulling on to the tarmac in front of the fence and parking behind a small red Peugeot.

'But Mr Sullivan says—'

'Mr Sullivan isn't trying to get you to school on time. Anyway, we'll just be a few minutes. The bell's about to go: hurry up.'

Both children took their own sweet time unbuckling the seatbelts and getting down from the car. Then Saffron noticed Aurora's laces were undone. 'Oh, for heaven's sake!' She knelt to tie them.

'Mum, I forgot my reading book,' said Chad. 'Can you—'

'No, I can't!' barked Saffron. 'Go to your lines before the bell rings.' She marched to the gate and held it open for them. 'Aurora, I'll talk to your teacher about your shoes.'

'Mrs Hanratty,' prompted Aurora.

'Yes, I know. Now go!'

''Scuse me.' It was a voice Saffron knew, and disliked intensely.

Standing halfway between the gate and the main entrance, arms folded in the manner of a bouncer, was Mr Sullivan, the school caretaker. 'Yes?'

'Those spaces are staff only at this time of day.' His face was neutral rather than angry, which somehow made her feel more as if she was being told off. By someone who was probably younger than she was.

'I'm sorry, I had no idea,' she said flatly.

'I'm pretty sure I've mentioned it to you, Mrs Montgomery.'

'Ms.'

'And it's been in the school newsletter more than once.'

She held up her hands. 'OK, I was in a rush.' *Unlike you, standing there in your scruffy jeans like the parking police.* He hadn't even shaved: his dark stubble was practically a beard.

'It's a matter of safety,' he said. 'I'd appreciate it if you could remember in future.'

By the time Saffron had thought of a suitably cutting reply, he was ambling to the school entrance. There was a big smear of green paint on his jeans. *What sort of example is that for the children?* Her eyes narrowed as she inspected his T-shirted top half. *Not to mention those sleeve tattoos.*

The bell rang, and she remembered the trainers. No doubt Mrs Hanratty would give her a lecture on uniform standards. If she did, Saffron was ready to give her a piece of her mind. She tossed her bouncy hair and stalked towards the junior playground, head held high.

2

As it turned out, Mrs Hanratty was surprisingly sympathetic. 'Kids always grow out of things at the most inconvenient time,' she said. 'Of course Roar can wear her trainers if her school shoes don't fit any more.'

Saffron considered correcting her about Aurora's name, but decided to be merciful in the circumstances and merely said 'Thank you.'

Mrs Hanratty glanced around the playground at the dispersing parents and leaned closer. 'As it's the last half term, we have a policy that the children can wear trainers. No sense in buying shoes they'll only grow out of at this point in the year. We're spending most of our time on the field or the playground anyway, as the weather's so nice. So they'll practically all be in trainers.'

'That's good to know,' said Saffron. 'A very

sensible policy, given that some parents must be feeling the pinch.'

'Quite,' said Mrs Hanratty. 'Well, better go and teach the little darlings, I suppose.'

'Yes, and I must get to work,' said Saffron. 'My clients won't look after themselves.'

'Saffron!'

She turned. It was Heather, happily married fellow-menace of the PTA, a businesswoman who was going places. Since her divorce, Saffron had mostly avoided her. Too painful a contrast. 'Oh, hello. How are you?'

'Oh, fine, fine. Would you like a coffee? I've heard about something that may interest you. I don't have to be online until ten today.'

'Um, let me check my schedule.' Saffron took out her phone and consulted her blank calendar. 'Go on then. Luckily, most of today's clients are transatlantic.' *Nonexistent.*

'Excellent,' Heather said briskly. 'Let's go.'

***

They went to Café de Paris, in the village. Denise, the owner, was behind the counter. She gave Heather a pleasant smile, then beamed at Saffron. 'Welcome back! Have you been working away?'

'In a manner of—'

'Two cappuccinos and two almond croissants, please,' said Heather. 'My treat.'

'You really don't have to—'

'We'll be over there.' Heather led the way to a round table with two bentwood chairs, each with a cushion in a fifties-style print of chic women walking dogs.

Saffron wondered what the opportunity might be. Presumably she would be doing Heather a favour, since she was being taken out for coffee and croissants. She hoped it wasn't compliance training, her least favourite. Though of course she'd do it.

She leaned forward. 'How are you? We see each other in passing at the PTA meetings, of course, but everything's so busy.'

'Oh yes?' Heather's eyebrows lifted slightly.

'You know how it is. Clients on the go, always switched on...' Saffron tried not to wriggle under Heather's scrutiny.

'Times are hard,' said Heather. 'Right now, I'm putting the hours in just to keep things at the same level.'

A young server arrived with a tray. 'Two cappuccinos, two croissants,' he said, setting out cups, plates and cutlery rolled in a napkin.

'Thank you,' said Heather, and smiled at him. 'Let's tuck in, shall we.'

Saffron broke a small piece from the end of the croissant and put it in her mouth. Her brain flooded with images: savouring a croissant at the breakfast bar at home, as a reward for leading a coaching seminar for a business in Germany. A treat bought in advance and consumed in bed after a talk on resilience delivered to a team in Sacramento. Late-night snack or very early breakfast, depending on your view. She had eaten in silence and darkness, not wanting to disturb David…

She looked at her plate. Half the croissant was gone. She picked up her cappuccino and sipped, then put it down. 'So, Heather, what can I do for you?'

'Do you know the little convenience store on the road to Meadborough? The Country Stores?'

Saffron frowned. She had seen the shop, on her way to Meadborough to get her nails done or catch a train to London, but had never visited it.

'It's on the corner. They have boxes outside with fruit and veg.'

'Yes, I know it.' Her eyebrows drew closer together and she made an effort to force them apart. If her frown lines deepened, there was no way she could get them fixed at the moment. What was Heather getting at? 'Is it part of a chain?'

'No, it's a husband and wife team. The kids used to help in the shop, but they live and work elsewhere now.'

'I don't see what—'

'Alf and Janet are getting on, and the shop's becoming too much for them. Janet fell off a kick stool when she was restocking the other day and sprained her ankle. I was in there buying emergency wellies – it's that kind of shop, sells everything – and they're desperate for a hand. But they don't want to go through the rigmarole of applications and interviews and all that.'

Saffron smiled. This was either a coaching assignment or a recruitment exercise. Fine. She could cope with that.

'I said I knew someone who might be able to help and told them I'd have a word.' Heather sipped her drink. 'So, would you be interested? It's within school hours, ten till two, Monday to Friday. They said they could pay eleven pounds an hour, maybe more for the right person.'

'Eleven pounds—' Saffron's jaw dropped. 'You mean you're asking me to – to work in the shop?'

'I know it isn't your usual line of work, Saffron,' said Heather. 'Alf said he'd be happy to show you the ropes. It's not like there would be systems to learn.'

'I – I—' For once, Saffron was speechless.

'Do you feel insulted?' Heather asked quietly. 'I'm sorry if you do. But you look as if you need help.'

'Not that sort of help,' snapped Saffron.

Heather reached for Saffron's hand and examined her nails. They were clipped instead of filed, painted with metallic bronze nail varnish which had gone clumpy and chipped at the tips. One nail was cut short. 'When was the last time you had a manicure?'

'I haven't had time!' Saffron wanted to cry. No, she wanted to run and hide where no one could catch sight of her or her raggedy nails and make assumptions.

'I know it's not what you're used to,' Heather said gently. 'Please think about it. I've recommended you, so they're bound to take you on. A steady job – an easy job – during school hours and out of the village. The chance of anyone from school seeing you is practically zero. And you could still do your own work around it, in the early mornings and the evenings.'

Saffron picked up her cappuccino and sat back. Eleven pounds an hour. Forty-four pounds a day. Over two hundred pounds a week, before tax. It would cover the shortfall in maintenance that was due to hit her next month.

'I didn't mean to, but I overheard your conversation with Mrs Hanratty,' said Heather. 'Times are hard for everyone, and if I can help…'

Saffron considered the alternative. Fewer companies were inviting pitches and tenders these days, and some of her most regular clients had either downsized or been absorbed into bigger companies with their own arrangements.

She saw herself buying the cheapest brands from the cheapest stores and refilling brand-name containers battered with use. Growing out her highlights. Telling the children that they couldn't go on the class trip because—

'I'll talk to them.' She seized the remains of her croissant and took a bite. But the croissant, which had always tasted of sweetness and sophistication and success before, was sickly and bitter. She took a swig of her cappuccino and managed to swallow it. Then she said 'Thank you,' which was even harder.

'It's a pleasure,' said Heather. 'We haven't seen as much of each other lately, but I couldn't help noticing, and I guess that the divorce—'

'Which was a good thing,' said Saffron. 'I'm better off without him.'

'Yes, I'm sure, but I imagine it can strain one's finances.'

As if you'd know, thought Saffron, eyeing Heather's perfect ombré French manicure and noting that the bag she'd dropped on the floor beside them was a Burberry.

'Anyway,' said Heather, 'I'd better make tracks. My ten o'clock's a bit tricky and I could do with prep time.'

'Sure,' said Saffron. 'You do you.'

Heather smiled. 'Let me know how it goes.' She leaned down for her bag, then rose and air-kissed Saffron. 'Good luck.'

'Thanks,' said Saffron, automatically.

She sat for some time after Heather had gone.

When the server came to clear the plates, the inch of cappuccino left in her cup was stone cold.

'Was everything all right?' he asked.

Saffron stared at him. She had thought she would be offered a nice package of work at a tempting day rate. Instead, Heather had thrown her a scrap. Working in a general store, for heaven's sake. A minimart. What would that do to her nails?

'With your drinks and—'

'Oh yes,' said Saffron hastily. 'Everything was fine, thanks.' She collected her bag, stood up, and strode out.

She had been offered a job she wouldn't have chosen in a million years. And she had no choice but to take it.

3

'There's nothing to it, really,' said Alf. 'Most of the stuff, you just scan the barcode. If there's no barcode, there should be a price sticker. If there's no price sticker, check the shelf. Once you've rung everything in, you press this button.' He obliged, and the till made a strange sound. A sort of cough, as if it couldn't quite believe what it was hearing. 'You ask if they're paying cash or card. If it's cash, you open the till…'

Saffron felt her mind wandering and snapped to attention.

'Take the cash, entering the amount, and that will tell you how much change to give.'

'And if it's card?'

'Which it is more and more these days. Or sometimes phone, or even smart watch. Like magic, it is. Provided you can get a signal…'

Saffron had considered going home to get changed after her meeting with Heather, since there was no point wasting a Boden top on a minimart. Then she thought *Why should I? They can take me as I am.* So she had merely refreshed her lip gloss in the car park, then jumped up and down a few times, to give herself energy and bounce, and walked in.

'Hello, pet,' said the elderly man behind the counter, who was reading the paper. Presumably, this was Alf. 'Is it windy out?'

'Er, no.' Saffron pushed her hair back.

'So what can I do you for?'

'My friend Heather told me you needed some help.' Saffron stuck out her hand. 'Saffron Montgomery.'

He looked at the hand, then her, and shook it with good grace. 'Hello, Saffron. Heather is the smart lady, isn't she? Always in a rush.'

'That's her,' said Saffron, though actually she thought Heather lacked dynamism.

He chortled. 'I shall feel like a magician with a glamorous assistant!' Before she could moderate that remark, he said, 'Did she tell you what was involved?'

'Yes. Ten till two, five days a week.'

'Can you lift a bag of logs?'

'I beg your pardon?'

'If you can't, it's not too much of a problem. Some customers like us to take it to the car for them, but I daresay we can work something out. A trolley, maybe.'

'Where are the bags?' said Saffron, drawing herself up.

He pointed. 'At the back, left-hand corner.'

Saffron marched through the shop, seized a bag by its scruff, hoisted it onto her shoulder and carried it to the cash register and back. She took her time putting it down, as she was slightly out of breath. 'Happy?' She resolved to practise with the dumbbells at home when the kids were in bed: she seemed to have lost strength since cancelling her gym membership.

Alf whistled. 'Very impressive.'

'Thanks.' Saffron brushed her hands together and strolled to the counter.

'Right, I'll give you the tour, as it's quiet. You've seen the fruit and veg out front. The rest of it is over there.' He gestured to wooden crates filled with cauliflowers, courgettes, and other seasonal produce. 'You'll need to weigh it, and the price per kilo is on here.' He pointed at a list taped to the counter. 'If something's bruised, just give it 'em.'

'Won't people take advantage of that?'

He shrugged. 'Maybe. If they're desperate enough to go to those lengths for a free tomato, I won't deny them.' He came out from behind the counter. 'Baked goods there, ready meals next door, tins in the next aisle, dairy section to the rear and there's a couple of freezers too. Pet supplies in the right-hand corner. Booze at the far end. Newspapers and magazines to the right. Sweets at the counter, with the freezer for ice creams and lollies. Ciggies and vapes behind me, either side of the door to the back of the shop, and here are the lottery tickets and scratch cards.'

'What do you do about ordering stock?' asked Saffron.

'I've got repeat orders set up for the basics. Local farmers and growers usually give us a ring when stuff's coming into season and we take it from there. Don't worry, that's Janet's department.'

'Oh yes,' said Saffron. 'Where is Janet?'

'At chair yoga,' said Alf. 'She's got a gammy leg, but she reckons she can manage that. Then she's helping out at the playgroup. Most days we take it turn and turn about in the shop, with an overlap at lunchtime. Now you're here, hopefully we can spend a bit more time together. Meet friends for lunch, take up some of those hobbies we always said we'd get round to.' He studied Saffron from under shaggy eyebrows. 'So, are you ready for the customers?'

'Oh yes,' said Saffron, with conviction. How hard could it be? She could work the cash register, she knew where everything was, and she'd demonstrated she could lift heavy items. She cracked her knuckles. 'Bring it on.'

'That's the spirit.' Alf reached behind him and

handed her a navy tabard. 'There you go. Ready for action.'

Saffron looked at the tabard as if she was holding a dead fish. 'Surely you don't expect me to wear this.'

'Shops are messy places,' said Alf. 'I wouldn't want you to ruin that nice top.'

Saffron considered, somewhat mollified by Alf's recognition of her top as a quality item. 'I suppose you have a point.' She ran her hand over the nylon, which made a nails-down-the-blackboard screech. 'I'll run the risk,' she said, hanging it on its peg.

Alf shrugged. 'Don't say I didn't warn you.' He looked at his watch. 'I make it five to ten. Cup of tea?'

'Do you have any fruit tea? I only drink caffeine at breakfast.'

'Jan's got camomile tea, would that do?'

'Oh yes, that will be lovely. No milk or sugar.'

Alf's face signalled his opinion of Saffron's beverage preferences. 'I'll see what I can do,' he said, and opened the door to the back.

Saffron lifted the wooden flap which separated the counter from the main shop, took her place behind the counter, and surveyed her new queendom. Vegetables, bread, ready meals, tins, sweets and drinks. *It's four hours a day*, she thought. *Everyone will be busy building empires or changing nappies. I don't even know anyone who lives this far out. If someone does come in, I can say I'm helping as a favour. Surely it can't be that bad.*

She heard Alf whistling and the clink of a teaspoon chasing a teabag round a mug. She hoped that was his teabag he was squeezing to death. *This is just till I get back on my feet. As soon as I do, I'll be gone quicker than you can say business transformation.* And she allowed herself a little smile.

4

Two hours later, Saffron wished she hadn't been so firm about her no-caffeine policy. She had circled the shop numerous times, assembling the contents of Mrs Dawson's shopping list. 'Oh no, not those tomatoes, I like the Napolina ones. Could you get the value baked beans? Those ones you've brought are very expensive. And I may have said wholemeal bread, but I meant spelt.' Saffron had rung everything in, watched Mrs Dawson turn her handbag out on the counter in pursuit of her purse, then count and double-check twenty-pound notes, and had just given her her change when Mrs Dawson remembered that she had forgotten olive oil and cocktail sticks. 'Oh, and once you've done those could you pack the bags and carry them to the car for me? I'm afraid I can't manage them myself.' She held up three hessian shopping bags.

Saffron felt as if her smile would crack her face.

She allowed herself a few choice thoughts as she roamed the store for the missing items, locating the cocktail sticks next to the gin, of all places.

Once the transaction was complete, she left Alf in charge and lugged the bags to the car park, then stood in the hot sun for five minutes waiting for Mrs Dawson to catch up. She sailed over. 'Sorry, my dear, I was having a word with young Alf.' She rummaged in her handbag again and handed Saffron her keys. 'It's the mushroom-coloured one.'

Saffron saw a classic, boxy Mercedes. 'Right,' she said, and loaded the shopping.

'Thank you so much,' said Mrs Dawson. 'Wait a moment.' She took out her purse and handed Saffron a pound coin. 'For your trouble.'

'You don't have to—' But Mrs Dawson was already opening her door. Saffron pocketed the coin and walked into the shop, shaking her head once she was out of view.

Other customers, by comparison, were easy to deal with – in terms of their purchases, at least. However, what should have been quick transactions never were. Everyone had opinions about the weather, the new pothole which had developed not a hundred yards away, the yellow line which had mysteriously appeared outside the community centre, whether Pink Lady or Jazz were the best apples... Often another customer would come in and join the conversation, which lengthened matters still more. At one point, four customers were standing at the counter, goods paid for and change given, still discussing whether the parking spaces by the leisure centre were bound by the same rules as those in the adjoining car park.

Saffron noted that Alf kept the chat going while rarely expressing an opinion himself. When asked, Saffron said what she thought, which was usually met with 'Oh. Well, as I said...' It was more like a game than a discussion: the sort of game where you have to keep all the plates spinning without letting one drop.

Around noon, there was a welcome lull. 'Enjoy it while it lasts,' said Alf. 'It won't be long before the lunch crowd come in. If you need a comfort break, the loo's in back.'

It felt wonderful to close the bathroom door behind her and be on her own for the first time in over two hours. Her hands smelt of coins and plastic. As she washed them, she studied herself in the mirror. The left side of her hair had turned the wrong way and her face was flushed. *Probably all that interaction.* She applied more lipgloss, then found a hair claw and twisted her hair up. At least her top was still clean, though she felt sweaty. *I'll have to buy industrial-strength deodorant. And take a shower as soon as I get home.*

When she came into the shop, Alf said 'Time for lunch.' He walked to the chilled cabinet and took out a ham salad sandwich.

'Oh,' said Saffron. 'I didn't bring anything with me.'

Alf opened the sandwich packet. 'Just grab something off the shelf.'

Saffron's eyes widened. 'Are you sure?'

Alf laughed. 'It's my shop.' He put the packet on the counter, extracted the sandwich and took a hefty bite.

'Thank you.' Saffron went to the cabinet and scanned the contents. Ham salad, cheese salad, egg and cress, BLT... *Salt, fat, carbs...* She inspected the boxed salads and eventually chose an egg salad with a sachet of dressing which she intended to ignore. The shelf label said £1.99. She took the box to the counter, got her bag and rummaged for her purse. 'Two pounds,' she said, putting the coins on the counter.

Alf goggled at her. 'What's that for?'

'Lunch, obviously.'

Alf looked at the money, then at Saffron. 'You don't have to pay for that. If you want to bring your lunch in future, that's fine.'

'Oh. Thanks.' She wasn't sure if Alf was amused or hurt by the situation. She picked up the money and went into the back room for a fork. 'Would you like a drink?' she called.

'Yes please,' Alf replied. 'Strong tea, milk, one sugar.'

Saffron filled the kettle, switched it on and sat down. Working in the shop was harder than she had thought. Not in terms of the work itself – that was hardly taxing – but in navigating what was expected of her. She had assumed that helping herself to the stock would be absolutely forbidden, and here was Alf inviting her to. And she hadn't been prepared for the small talk, the endless small talk… Pretending to be interested in potholes and Mr Jones's begonias and Mrs Watson's collie's stomach—

The kettle clicked off and Saffron realised she hadn't got out mugs, teabags or anything. She hunted in the cupboard above the sink and it was only when she had filled both mugs with hot water that she saw she had given herself a normal teabag. She stared at it in dismay, then shrugged. *It won't kill me. Lord knows I could do with a boost.*

5

Saffron returned with the tea to find Alf chatting with a customer.

'Thanks, pet,' he said, and faced the customer. 'So, are you entering a marrow this year?'

'I'm undecided,' said the customer, a middle-aged man in a checked shirt and jeans. 'I don't have any obvious contenders at the moment. They're all a bit diddy.'

'Can't you feed one up?' asked Saffron. 'Not that I have any idea about growing prize marrows.'

'I could,' said the man. 'But it's a commitment. I might have to sacrifice the others, and there's the danger that it might get nobbled.'

Saffron laughed, then realised he was serious. 'People nobble prize vegetables?'

'It does happen,' said the customer. 'My dad was known for his giant veg, and if he had a really special one, he'd sleep with it for a week before the judging.'

Saffron struggled to keep her face straight. 'I see,' she said, and took refuge in her tea. She sipped, and the hot liquid spread through her veins. She noted wryly that fruit tea didn't have that effect.

'Well, good luck, Jeff, whatever you decide,' said Alf.

'Indeed,' said Jeff. He turned to Saffron. 'Are you a new member of staff?'

'We're trying each other out,' said Alf.

'Yes, we are,' said Saffron, and smiled at Jeff. 'See you again.'

Alf finished his sandwich and went through to the back room with the packaging. When he returned, he asked, 'So, how are you finding it?'

'It's fine,' said Saffron. 'I didn't think people would chat so much.' Then she recalled what Alf had said to Jeff: *We're trying each other out*. Had he introduced her to anyone today? Said she was working here? No, he hadn't. She faced him square on. 'Is there a problem?'

'No, not at all,' said Alf. 'It's just that . . . you don't seem to be enjoying yourself.'

'Oh, I am,' said Saffron. 'I have one of those faces. You know, when you don't look happy even though you are.' She picked up her mug, not exactly to hide behind it.

'Oh, you mean resting bitch face.'

Saffron nearly spat out her tea. 'How do you know about that?'

'Sometimes I flick through one of Jan's magazines,' said Alf, grinning. Then he became serious. 'If the work isn't to your liking, you can say.'

Saffron drank some more tea, to give herself time to think.

Is this what I want to do for four hours every weekday? No.

Do I need the money? Yes.

'This job isn't quite what I thought it would be,' she said. 'But I'm confident I can learn, and if you have any feedback for me, I'd be happy to hear it.'

Alf raised his eyebrows. 'You sure?'

'Of course.' Saffron braced herself.

'In that case...' Alf took a swig of tea. 'Relax, Saffron. You're stiff as a board when you're dealing with the customers, and they can tell. They won't mind if you make a mistake: you're new.'

'Have I made a mistake?'

'No, you've been spot on, and you've remembered all the things I told you. Look, what's your normal line of work?'

Saffron searched for words to explain it in a way that Alf could understand. 'I work with businesses and teams to implement transformational change. Sometimes it's through individual coaching, sometimes with team workshops—'

'A management consultancy sort of thing?'

'Yes,' said Saffron, surprised.

'So you'll understand what I mean when I say that a lot of my customers aren't here for beans and a newspaper. They're here for a chat. Some don't get out much and I'm a friendly face, as is Janet. Some of them make a pitstop between rushing from meeting to meeting, or before dashing home to put their kids to bed. Coming in gives them a chance to switch from business to family mode, so to speak. Even if they just say "Hello, Alf" and we talk about the weather for two minutes. They could stop off at Tesco during the day, or get stuff delivered to their house, but they don't. They come here. In our own way, we're providing a little experience.'

'Understood,' said Saffron. 'So you want me to make conversation with the customers.'

'I just want you to relax, then it will come naturally. You were fine with Jeff, because you were curious about his marrows. It'll be easier when you get to know a few of them.'

'OK,' said Saffron. 'I'll eat my salad before the rush.' She speared a bit of lettuce and half a cherry tomato, put it in her mouth and chewed vigorously. Then she sighed, opened the little sachet of dressing and squeezed it over the rest of the salad. The next mouthful was better. *I am not going to fail*, she told herself. *This is the most basic job I've ever had. I will not be let go*. She forked in mouthful after mouthful, chewing away, until the container was empty. 'Right.' She marched towards the back room with the box.

'For what it's worth,' said Alf, 'you've picked everything up really well. You've been here, what, two hours, and I wouldn't have a problem with nipping out and leaving you in charge.'

'Oh. Good.' She paused. 'Um, what do I do with this? Is there recycling?'

'Yup. Leave it on the side through there and I'll deal with it.'

Saffron did as she had been instructed then washed her hands. As she was drying them, she heard Alf say 'How do, Jamie?'

'Not bad, Alf,' said a vaguely familiar voice.

'How's she coming along?'

'Fits and starts.'

Saffron wondered if they were talking about another giant vegetable. She opened the door to find Mr Sullivan, the caretaker. 'Shouldn't you be at school?' she blurted.

'Lunch break.' He studied her. 'Shouldn't you be organising jumble sales, or fundraising for sports kits?'

'I'm lending a hand in the shop,' she said. 'For a while.'

'That's right,' said Alf. 'This is Saffron's first day with us, and she's doing well.'

'I'm sure *Saffron* is.' He gave her a sly glance. 'A woman with her skills should be an asset to your shop.' She couldn't work out if that was a compliment or an insult.

'I didn't know you knew each other,' said Alf.

'Our paths cross sometimes on the school run,' Saffron said. She eyed his purchases. 'I'm surprised you've come all this way for a BLT and a Coke.'

'It's the excellent service,' said Mr Sullivan. She would *not* think of him as Jamie. He held a card to the machine. The scales of the two fish tattooed on his forearm rippled as the muscles moved. She hadn't noticed before, but the scales were beautifully shaded, ranging from navy to pale orange. He saw her looking, and grinned. 'Admiring my fish?'

'Wondering how long it took to get them,' said Saffron.

'A few visits,' he said. 'I figured the end result was worth it.' He gathered his lunch and the fish rippled again. 'See ya, Alf.'

'Bye, Jamie.' Alf raised a hand as Jamie loped off.

Saffron reached for her mug and found it empty. 'More tea?'

'Don't mind if I do,' said Alf.

The afternoon was busy but uneventful, compared to the morning. Janet turned up, a small slight woman full of apologies, ate a ham salad in the intervals of talking, and left ten minutes later to go to Women's

Circle. By quarter to two, Saffron was exhausted from keeping her shoulders down, appearing relaxed, and resisting the urge to initiate conversations and push her opinion. *It's like anti-networking*, she thought. *Hang back, not lean in.*

Alf, who had been pottering round the shelves, returned with a hotchpotch of tins and jars. 'These have got short dates. Can you mark them down to half price? Take a couple, if you want. The pricing gun's under the counter: I'll show you what to do.'

Are you sure? was on the tip of Saffron's tongue. Instead, she said 'Thanks.'

She got to work with the pricing gun, which was surprisingly satisfying, and had the whole collection repriced in a few minutes. She had dismissed most of the tins – the soup would be too salty, tinned ham beyond the pale - but she did pause at the artichoke hearts. Those were definitely out of her reach at their usual price. And she loved artichokes. 'I'll pay you for these.'

'No need,' said Alf. 'Tell me what you cook with them and we'll put a recipe suggestion on the shelf. Don't know why I keep them in, really. I sell a jar once in a blue moon.'

'All right,' said Saffron. 'You're on.'

Alf grinned. 'Bet you didn't think you'd be getting homework. Speaking of which, it's five past two. Off you pop. I'll see you tomorrow.'

'Yes, see you tomorrow.' Saffron got her bag and hurried to the car, clutching her artichoke hearts.

The shower was every bit as welcome as she had anticipated. Saffron rotated beneath the warm water, trying to keep her hair from getting wet. Was she tired? Yes. Had it been as awful as she thought it would be? No. *I'll give it a week. Then I'll know.*

6

And so it began. Every morning, Saffron rose bright and early, did stretching exercises and some light weights, and got ready for the school run before chivvying the children through breakfast, uniforms, and school bags. She had taken to calling them a bit earlier so that they could walk to school, thus avoiding any more confrontations with Mr Sullivan and his tattooed fish.

Once the children were safely in their classrooms, she hurried home and swapped her tight jeans, posh top and heeled boots for wide-leg pants, a T-shirt and trainers. After seeing the state of her nails at the end of the first day, she had trimmed them into short squovals and put on clear varnish. She made sure she had a scrunchie or a hair claw with her, then headed to work.

When she came home, Saffron had a quick shower

and transformed into her usual go-getting deal-making self in time for the school run. This was done in the car, firstly because Aurora and Chad would have after-school activities – swimming, football or a play date – and secondly because after four hours on her feet, she felt she deserved to sit down.

Somehow, she had become the shop's resident chef. She had used the tin of artichoke hearts to make creamy artichoke and spinach pasta, and the children had actually eaten it. Chad had asked what the squidgy things were, but when Saffron replied 'Chopped zombie brains,' that seemed to satisfy him. In fact, he had a second helping.

'Knew you'd manage to do something with them,' said Alf. He rummaged under the counter and produced a large shelf label. 'Write a summary and let's see if we can shift some more.' He tapped the basket of tins on the counter, against which was propped a piece of card saying *HALF PRICE*. 'If you can work out any recipes for what's in there, help yourself and write them up afterwards. I could stop stocking those lines, but I don't like the idea of not having a product that people might want.'

Saffron's brain buzzed with phrases: *Meet the customer where they are*, *Go for the low-hanging fruit* and *Don't spread yourself too thinly*, but she sensed Alf was not about to change his mind. Instead, she browsed the basket and pulled out a dented can of new potatoes. 'I may have an idea for these.' That night she made warm new potato salad and scored another hit.

Once she had recovered from the shock of the first day, work became much easier. She was less focused on not making mistakes, and able to listen to the customers. She remembered a couple of their names and asked after Mrs Watson's collie, who was much better on the Chappie, thank you.

On the third day, Alf disappeared around ten o'clock to work on his allotment. A few minutes later, Janet came in.

'How's the ankle?' Saffron asked.

'Not bad,' said Janet. 'Think my gymnastics days are done.' She grinned. 'You've settled in.'

'Thanks.'

'There isn't much to it,' said Janet. 'It's just keeping the place ticking over. Speaking of which, do you mind if I nip out? I've got a couple of parcels to take to the post office and I'd like to get them in before noon.'

'Yes, of course,' said Saffron. 'That's fine.'

'I'll leave you my mobile number, just in case.'

'I'm sure everything will be—'

But Janet was already scribbling on the small notepad they kept on the counter. 'There you go,' she said, pushing it towards Saffron. 'Put it in your phone, then you won't lose it. What did we do without mobile phones?'

Saffron, who had seen Janet's ancient pink Nokia, merely smiled. 'I know,' she said.

'I shouldn't be too long,' said Janet. 'Unless there's a queue. And I might pop to the library while I'm in town, for that book I requested. Tell you what, if you need me, give me a ring. Alf will probably be back at lunchtime, anyway. Unless he meets one of his gardening pals down the allotment and goes for a pint. Anyway, catch you later.'

As the shop was empty, Saffron allowed herself a big stretch and went to put the kettle on. Automatically, she reached for the PG Tips. The tea made, she strolled around her domain, noting gaps on the shelves, moving stock forward and generally tidying up.

The bell on the door rang and she turned. 'Oh. Hello.'

'Hello,' said Jamie Sullivan. 'Still here, then.'

'I'm holding the fort,' said Saffron. 'Alf and Janet are both out.' She checked her watch. 'Isn't it a bit early for lunch?'

'Day off.' He wandered to the chilled cabinet.

Saffron studied him. He looked just as scruffy as on working days, if not more so. His stubble was darker than usual, his jeans had acquired new black and blue stains and his navy T-shirt was speckled with white. Not that she was examining him with any interest, of course. *Is he painting the whole school? Why doesn't he wear overalls?* Then she glanced at the nylon tabard hanging on its peg and shrugged.

He chose a cheese sandwich and a Diet Coke, which he supplemented with a pack of roast beef Monster Munch. He brought it all to the counter. 'Can I ask you something, Saffron?'

'Ms Montgomery,' she shot back.

He rolled his eyes. 'All right, *Ms* Montgomery. Do your kids know you're working here?'

Heat rushed over Saffron like a forest fire. 'No, they don't!' she snapped. 'This is a temporary job, so they don't need to know. I'm just filling in while – while…'

'There's nothing to be ashamed of.'

'I didn't say there was. But this isn't my usual line of work, and I have no intention of pursuing it for longer than necessary.'

'So it's necessary?'

She studied the counter, unable to meet his eyes. 'For the moment, yes.' She grabbed the sandwich and scanned it, then the drink and crisps. 'Have a nice day.'

'I intend to.' He didn't move. *Why won't he pick up his stuff, get out and leave me in peace?* 'I'm sorry things aren't going well.'

'Things are fine. It's just a temporary lull. Happens in business sometimes.'

'Mmm.' He looked at her. 'Give us a scratch card, would you.'

'Any particular kind?'

'You choose.'

She pursed her lips and considered the options. Nothing stood out, so she chose one at random, garish in yellow and green, and scanned it.

He touched a card to the reader, then picked up his lunch. 'Cheers.'

He was halfway to the door before she realised. 'You forgot your scratch card,' she called.

He looked round. 'That's for you. Maybe your luck will change.' He left, whistling.

Saffron stuffed the scratch card in her handbag, her face burning. *Who does he think he is?* As if a scratch card would change anything. She didn't need luck: she needed an opportunity. The right client would come along – the right *clients* – and everything would go back to normal. *I must work on my manifestation skills. And start putting bids in again.* She stalked to the chiller cabinet and rearranged the sandwiches to fill the gap he had left.

7

Saffron made it through the first week, then the second. She found herself waking before the alarm and wondering who would come in that day. Would Jeff have an update on his marrow, now that he had decided to go for it? How many circuits of the shop would she have to make if Mrs Dawson came in with her list? Which sandwich would Jamie Sullivan choose today?

Sometimes she wandered around the shop, noting unusual foods she could do something with. Alf and Janet always told customers what Saffron had made with various ingredients – tired courgettes which had gone into a parmigiana, tinned ham and leek pie, cauliflower cheese fritters, beetroot hummus – and often customers picked up the item and said they would give it a go. Saffron had begun writing out the recipes so that people could take a picture with their phones. It reminded her of her student days, when she'd made huge pots of stew and veg chilli for her housemates – anything that would fill them up on a budget.

The random assortment of food which Alf and Janet pressed on her had definitely got her out of her cooking rut. Before, it had been a cycle of pasta with sauce and hidden vegetables, veggie burgers and wholemeal buns, mild chicken curry with rice... Perhaps, finally, Aurora and Chad were becoming the adventurous eaters she had always hoped they would be.

She doubted there was any need to exercise in the mornings now, as she got plenty of stretching and weights practice at the shop. But she felt better for it, and the earlier starts meant she could fit in yoga too.

One morning she made French toast for the children, since she had time and an egg to use. Chad wolfed his down. Aurora took a bite then looked at Saffron, a little furrow between her eyebrows.

'What's up?' asked Saffron. 'Don't you like it?'

'I'll eat it if Roar doesn't want it,' said Chad.

'It's lovely, Mummy,' said Aurora. 'Is today a special day?'

'Not particularly,' said Saffron. 'I just thought I'd make a different breakfast.'

'Oh,' said Aurora. She took another bite of the toast. 'Are you shopping at another supermarket?'

'Aurora, you saw the van park outside the other day and you helped me put the food away. You know it's the same supermarket.'

'Something's different,' said Aurora. She took a big bite of her toast, swinging her legs as she chewed.

At the end of the first week, Saffron was surprised when Alf opened the till, counted out some notes and slid them across the counter. 'There you go. Twenty hours at twelve pounds an hour makes two hundred and forty.'

Saffron looked at the money, then picked it up. 'Thank you. I wasn't expecting cash.'

'Well, I *could* ask you for a load of information and fill out all the forms, but I figured you'd rather have the money now. We can sort it out later, if we have to.'

Saffron put the money in her purse, wished him a good weekend and headed to her car. It was only when she was almost home that she realised Alf had paid her more than she expected. Twelve pounds an hour, not eleven. Her throat tightened. *He didn't have to do that*, she thought, and blinked hard.

That weekend, she used some vouchers she had forgotten about and took Aurora and Chad to see the latest Pixar film. She couldn't run to cinema snacks, but she smuggled in bottles of pop and home-made chocolate brownies. She couldn't remember the last time they had gone to the cinema. Probably not since the – since David had moved out of the house and in with *her*. Saffron had been too busy keeping her business going, and lately, she hadn't had the money to spare.

Halfway through the third week, Saffron was alone in the shop, standing on the kick stool and restocking the tinned veg, when the shop bell rang. 'Hello!' she called. 'Do you need any help?'

'I'm looking for vanilla essence,' said a woman's voice.

'It's with the flour in the second aisle,' Saffron called. Then she frowned. *I know that voice.* In her head, she ran through a list of the shop's regulars. It was none of those. The voice was . . . not local. Well spoken, slightly older than her.

'Got it,' said the voice, and heels clicked towards her. 'Can I pay, pl— Oh, it's you!'

Saffron froze. Diana Hargreaves, veteran of a thousand business breakfasts and coaching seminars, was standing in front of her, holding a bottle of vanilla essence and grinning. 'I hardly recognised you in your tabard,' she said.

'What? Oh.' She was only wearing the tabard because Janet had asked if she could come in half an hour early and there wasn't time to change out of the Whistles top she had worn for the school run. There would have been, but she had chatted about a PTA fundraiser with a couple of mums on the playground.

Then Jamie Sullivan had caught her as she was leaving to ask whether her 4x4 was petrol or diesel, and how it did for fuel economy. And here she was, with her hair skewered up anyhow and resplendent in a nylon tabard, standing on a kick stool like a monument to shop workers.

She bundled the tins she was holding onto the shelf and climbed down. 'I don't work in this shop, not really. The owner's poorly at the moment, so I said I'd help.'

Diana laughed. 'You certainly look the part. I wondered why I hadn't seen you at Motivation Monday lately.'

I can't afford it. 'I couldn't make it. Booked solid.'

'Oh, that's good,' Diana said easily.

Saffron suspected she didn't believe a word of it. 'Yes, and I must admit that doing this is cramping my style. As soon as the owner's back on her feet, I'll be on the circuit again. I just couldn't leave her in the lurch. Little shops like this are so important for the community, aren't they?'

'Oh yes,' said Diana. 'Now, if I could pay?'

'Of course.' Saffron hurried to the counter. The quicker the transaction was over, the sooner Diana would be gone. 'Cash or card?'

Diana gave her a pitying glance and took out her phone.

Saffron rang up the sale. 'When you're ready.'

Diana touched her phone to the reader. 'What will you be making?'

'I won't.' Diana dropped the little bottle in her bag. 'Minerva is making biscuits in food tech.' She smiled at Saffron. 'Maybe you should keep the tabard: it suits you. See you soon.' She clicked her way to the door.

Seething, Saffron returned to the shelves and shoved the tins into place. What a thing to happen. Hopefully, Diana wouldn't gossip. Hopefully, she was so busy that the encounter would drop out of her head, not to be recalled until Saffron was back on top of her game. Whenever that might be. She hadn't even thought about clients, bids or tenders since starting work at the Country Stores.

Saffron stepped down and nudged the kick stool into the corner with her foot. *Don't get too comfortable*, she told herself, then took off the tabard and hung it on its peg. *This isn't where you belong*. She resolved to get on her laptop and explore opportunities as soon as the kids were settled in bed that evening. Once she'd written up that night's recipe.

8

'So, what are you doing at school today?'

Aurora looked confused. 'Don't you remember, Mummy? It's the school trip!'

'School trip? What school trip?' Saffron had a vision of arriving at school with her daughter to find a coach ready to go and no place for Aurora on it. 'Where to? Was there a letter? Did you bring home a letter? Or was it on the app? I didn't see anything.'

'I brought it home ages ago,' said Aurora. 'We're doing a traffic survey in Meadley. For our topic.'

'Oh. Oh yes.' Saffron closed her eyes and monitored her breathing for a few seconds. 'Do you need anything? A packed lunch? Money?'

'We're having lunch at school as usual, Mummy. Mrs Hanratty said we could bring a pound, so I've got one from my money box.'

'Oh. OK.' Saffron studied her daughter. Usually,

Aurora had no idea what was going on. This was a welcome development. 'So, all sorted, then. Just make sure you're careful around the roads, and do as Mrs Hanratty tells you. What are you doing today, Chad?'

Chad shrugged. 'English. Maths. Something in the afternoon.'

Saffron sighed. At least one of them was up to speed.

She walked the children in and saw them to their respective lines, saying hello to various mums on the way. She wondered where they shopped, what they bought, what they cooked, how much they spent…

'Hello there, *Ms* Montgomery.' It was Jamie, the caretaker. He leaned on the Ms to annoy her, she was sure. 'Nice day for it.'

Saffron looked up. The sky showed a gradient of pale to deeper blue, with a couple of candy-floss clouds to break the monotony. 'Yes, it is.' She smiled. 'A good day for a school trip.'

'Oh, is one of yours off out?'

'Yes, on a traffic survey. I'd better get on.' She glanced about: no one was near. 'The shelves won't stack themselves.'

He grinned. 'Bet you wish they would.' His eyebrows drew together slightly. 'Which one of yours is going on the trip?'

'Aurora, in year five. Mrs Hanratty's class.' He didn't answer. 'I assume you'll be in for your customary sandwich later,' she said, and went on her way.

She glanced back at the gate, and saw him striding towards the school entrance. Her gaze settled on his bottom. *Nice to see you getting a move on for once, Jamie*, she thought, and smirked.

As she drove to the Country Stores, she pondered the mystery of Jamie Sullivan. Why did he come all the way out of Meadley to Alf's shop? He'd have to drive, and there was a petrol station not five minutes' walk from the school which sold perfectly adequate sandwiches. Not that she'd ever eaten one, but they looked OK.

Unless he lives over this way... But in that case, why didn't he call in on his way to work? Or if the shop wasn't open, why not on his way home? That would be a much better use of his time.

She was coming to the double bend in the road, and focused on her driving until she was safely through it. From this point, Meadley opened up into fields and farmland, in the midst of which was The Country Stores. Saffron pulled into the car park, got out and stood for a moment, admiring the view. Beyond the low wooden fence were open fields, with distant, smudgy hills and an occasional spreading tree. In autumn, there would probably be mist. *Lots of people would pay good money for a view like that.* She wondered if Alf and Janet thought much of it.

Then she looked at her watch, a Gucci with a fraying strap, and hurried inside.

Today, Alf was behind the counter. Leaning on it, to be precise. 'Morning,' said Saffron. 'How are you?'

'I've been better,' said Alf, and winced. 'I've pulled my back.'

'Oh no. Have you taken painkillers?'

'I'm waiting to see if it – *ow* – goes off.'

'Oh, *men*.' Saffron opened her bag and found a strip of paracetamol. 'Take two of these, at least.' On the shelves, she found a tube of Deep Heat and a self-heating back wrap. 'Should you be working?' she asked, as she put them on the counter.

'Didn't have a choice. Jan's got an early appointment at the hairdresser and I can't let down the customers.'

'Well, I'm here now…' She paused. 'Speaking of customers, why does Jamie Sullivan come in every day for his lunch? There's loads of other shops nearer the school.'

Alf eased two paracetamol from the blister pack and gulped them with the rest of his tea. 'Maybe it's the excellent service. Maybe he fancies a change of scene. Maybe it's something else.' He twinkled at her. 'And maybe you should ask him, not me.'

'Thanks for nothing,' said Saffron. 'Want another tea?'

'Please. And if you wouldn't mind bringing a chair

with you…'

Saffron fetched a chair and Alf lowered himself carefully into it, landing with an *oof* and another wince. 'How did you pull your back?'

Alf looked shifty. 'I was fetching a sack of sawdust. I twisted to get it through the door, and bingo.'

'I did say you should use a trolley.'

'I suppose,' Alf said, resentfully. 'In my head, I'm still in my twenties. I could have carried three of those then and thought nothing of it.'

'Did you work here in your twenties?'

'I did. My parents owned this place and I was more than happy to take it on. Shame the kids weren't keen.' He shifted slightly in the chair. 'Now, that tea…'

'On it, boss,' she said, and went through to the back.

When she returned with two strong cups of PG Tips, Alf had a list of jobs for her. 'Normally this is done before you turn up,' he said. 'But I decided to do the sawdust first and everything went pear shaped.'

'Just tell me what needs doing, and I'll get to it between customers.'

'First job is to sort out the sack of sawdust stuck in the doorway to the storeroom. Don't even think about lifting it, or you might be on the sick list too. It needs putting in smaller bags. I'll let you work out how best to do it, but I'm telling you now, put the tabard on. That stuff gets everywhere.'

Dealing with the sawdust took a good forty minutes, since it was punctuated by having to dash to the counter and serve people, who all wanted to know why Alf was sitting down and offered various remedies as well as the usual updates and enquiries about today's recipe (fish-finger curry à la Nigella Lawson). Saffron felt as if she was trapped in some sort of Groundhog Day situation as yet another customer said 'What's with the chair, Alf?'

After that, she got on with filling gaps in the shelves, checking for fallen labels, and tidying the chilled cabinet. She was organising the sandwiches when the shop bell rang.

She looked round. 'Typical,' she said, grinning. 'Just as I get this cabinet in order, you come in to mess it up.'

'Nice to see you too,' said Jamie. 'Anyway—'

'You're bright and early. Another day off? No, it can't be – I saw you in the playground.'

'I'm here to tell you something. I'd have come earlier, but a piece of play equipment needed fixing.'

'You've come to tell me something?' She smiled, intrigued.

'The school trip your daughter's on—'

The bell rang as Mrs Hanratty entered the shop. Saffron's jaw dropped. 'Good morning, Alf. Why are you sitting down? Having a rest before the onslaught?' Then she turned. 'Come along, children, we can't stay too long or we'll be late for lunch. Remember, no one is to spend more than a pound. Make your choice quickly, then bring it to the counter and Mr Smith will serve you.'

Children began to file in, tentatively at first. Saffron recognised several of them. *This can't be happening.* She hurried to the rear of the shop and peeped round the shelf. The children had spotted the sweets and converged there, chattering and shrieking. And there was Aurora, coming in with her friend Chloe, with Mrs Luckhurst the teaching assistant bringing up the rear.

She heard footsteps and shrank back. 'Mrs H does this trip every year,' Jamie murmured, 'and she always finishes here.'

Saffron closed her eyes. She felt as if the ceiling might fall on her.

'Stay there,' said Jamie, and strode to the counter. 'Need a hand, Alf? No, don't get up. Just tell me what to do.'

Several of the children said 'Hello, Mr Sullivan,' and Saffron slowly let out a breath.

'Where's Saffron?' said Alf. 'She ought to be serving. Saffron!'

Saffron straightened, uncertain what to do, and glanced at Jamie for guidance. But a voice said

'That's my mummy's name!' and Aurora half ran down the aisle. 'Mummy!' she cried. 'What are you doing here? And why are you wearing a – a shop uniform?'

Jamie reached Saffron first. 'I did try,' he said, putting a hand on her arm.

'I know.' Her breath was coming in gasps. She could hear children whispering, 'That's Roar's mum.'

'Guess you'll have to fess up,' he said, softly.

'Why are you talking to Mr Sullivan? You don't *like* him.' Aurora's voice rang out, clear as a bell. 'And why are you wearing that thing? You don't work here...' Aurora gazed around the shop, at the tins and packets and vegetables and Saffron's handwritten shelf labels, and it was as if a lightbulb switched on above her head. 'Mummy!'

'I—' Saffron swallowed. She looked past Aurora to the counter. Alf was staring at her with a face full of disappointment.

'Go to Mrs Hanratty, Aurora,' she said. 'Choose some sweets.'

'But why—'

'Just go!'

'Thanks a bunch,' said Jamie, and strode towards the counter.

Saffron ripped at the straps of the tabard with a great tearing of Velcro, flung it on the floor, and ran out of the shop. As she rushed to the car, images flicked through her head like playing cards dealt in a pile over and over: Aurora's horror, Alf's disappointment, Jamie's contempt. Horror, disappointment, contempt. And she couldn't fix any of it. She was all out of solutions.

9

Saffron had just reached the car when she realised the major flaw in her escape plan. Her keys, phone and purse were in her bag, which was behind the shop counter.

I can't go back. Not after – that.
But you can't stay here.
I can't face Aurora. Never mind the rest of them.

She recalled that Mrs Hanratty had told the children they couldn't stay long, and Jamie would have to return to school at some point. If she waited until they had gone…

There was literally nowhere to go. The shop was surrounded by fields, and the few buildings within walking distance were at the end of long drives. She imagined herself hiding in a barn, possibly amongst bales of hay. Then she looked at the 4x4 and the low fence beyond. She scrambled over the fence, sank down and put her head in her hands.

What was I thinking? I've been such a fool.

No doubt the children would talk about her on their walk. *It'll be all over the school by home time, and every parent on the PTA will know.* She sniffed, and blinked hard.

If I hadn't made a secret of the shop, I could have put my own spin on it. I could have said I was taking a break. Pivoting. Now everyone will know I work there because I can't make ends meet in my own business.

Which is the truth. Maybe I'm just not good enough at what I do to earn a living in these difficult times. Maybe I was kidding myself all those years, holding forth about clients and journeys and delighting the customer. She certainly hadn't done that today.

She heard high voices chattering in the distance, then the raised voice of Mrs Hanratty, telling the children to stay in pairs and not cross the road till they were told it was safe. Gradually, the voices died away.

What must Aurora think?

I even lied to my children. Well, perhaps I didn't tell them the whole truth—

You lied to them. You told them you were meeting clients when you were working in the shop. That's nothing to be ashamed of: it's honest work that needs doing. They trust you, and look what you did.

I'm a terrible parent…

She curled in a ball and cried, quietly. *If I could change the last quarter of an hour…*

But it goes back further than that. To my attitude, my snobbishness, my belief that I was too good to work in a shop. And it turns out the shop is too good for me.

'Your tractor's still here, so I assume you are too.'

It was Jamie's voice, but there was no warmth in it. 'The children have left and I'm about to, so the coast is clear for you to fetch your bag. I suggest you apologise to Alf while you're there.'

No more banter in the shop, she thought, *and no more chats on the playground.*

She heard the click of a car unlocking, the slam of the door, the growl of an engine.

A minute later, he was gone.

Saffron sat for a while, numb. Then she sighed and got to her feet. Despite the weather, she was shaky, stiff and chilly. Every step towards the shop felt like a step towards her execution.

When she entered, the shop bell rang as if she was just another customer. Alf, still sitting down, glanced her way.

'I'm sorry,' she said. 'I didn't mean—'

Alf held up a hand. 'It's not fair to run out of the shop and leave me with a load of kids. Not with this back.'

'I promise I'll nev—'

'Before you start making promises I'm not sure you'll keep, I've texted Jan and she's coming as soon as her hair's set, or whatever they do to it. So you don't need to stay.'

'I want to.'

'You didn't a few minutes ago.'

'I really am sorry.'

Alf didn't reply, or even look at her, and after a few moments she slunk out.

It took two goes to get her key in the ignition. She hoped the roads were quiet: she was in no fit state to drive. *I want to go home.* But home meant going through the village, and it was getting towards lunchtime. Cars would be crawling through, searching for somewhere to park, while people ambled across the road… She shivered at the thought that someone who knew what had happened would see her.

Saffron drove away from the village and parked in a little lay-by beside the river. *What a mess I've made of everything. It's as if the world's against me.*

No: it's you. You're your own worst enemy. None of this would have happened if it wasn't for your stupid pride. Over what? Your disappearing clients and your nonexistent business? Your fancy clothes, until they wear out? This gas-guzzling monster?

She glared at the huge dashboard and remembered Jamie asking about her car's fuel consumption. *If I hadn't messed up, maybe I could have sold it to him.* She pinched the bridge of her nose. *I could still trade it in and get a runabout.*

She closed her eyes and sighed. *Why didn't I think of all this before? And the house eats money.* She tried to tell herself that it was their family home, that she had to keep it for the children's sake, but in truth it felt more like a show home. It was a big house on a good road in a sought-after location: a polished, empty shell. *I'll talk to David about selling it and finding something smaller*, she thought. *But not today.*

She sighed and started the engine.

***

When Saffron drove back to the Country Stores, the car park was empty. She marched to the shop to get it over with. Hopefully it would be like ripping off a plaster: painful, but brief.

Janet was standing behind the counter, looking through a list, with Alf sitting next to her. No customers were near. 'I've come to apologise,' Saffron said. 'Properly. I've been a complete fool and I should have known better. I let pride get the better of me.'

'Alf told me what happened earlier,' said Janet. Her tone was neutral but her expression was set to stern. 'We can't employ an assistant who runs out of the shop, whatever the reason is.'

'I promise I'll never do it again,' said Saffron, 'no matter what happens.'

'You say that now,' said Alf. 'How do we know we can trust you?'

'All I can do is promise. And show you, through hard work.'

Alf considered this. 'You're a good worker, Saffron. I didn't think you would be when you first came. I thought you were too posh to get your hands dirty. I wasn't sure you'd last the week, but you proved me wrong. I assumed you were doing this for a bit of extra cash. Playing at shops.'

'I was at first,' said Saffron. 'I thought it would be easy, and that the work was beneath me. But it isn't,' she added, as Janet bristled. 'To begin with, I saw this job as a way to make easy money till my proper business was back on its feet.'

Janet raised her eyebrows. 'Your proper business?'

'Business consultancy.' Janet's nose wrinkled. 'But working here has made me think differently. I'd like to stay. If you'll have me.'

Alf harrumphed. 'You've apologised, we know you can do the job, and I don't want to have to look for a new assistant—'

'Thank you!' Saffron dived behind the counter and hugged him.

'Steady on!' he said, laughing. 'It's up to Jan as well, not just me.'

'I haven't seen as much of you as Alf has,' said Janet. 'But if he says you're a good worker, I'm prepared to give you another chance.'

'You won't regret it,' said Saffron. 'I promise.' She paused. 'What would you like me to do?' She scanned the shop for gaps to fill, shelves to tidy, surfaces to wipe...

'Go home,' said Alf. 'There's less than an hour of your shift left, and if you haven't already, you should think about what you'll say to your kid. And her teacher.' He raised his eyebrows. 'Not to mention young Jamie. He stayed to help while the kids were here, and while he managed to smile at them, I could tell he was fuming.'

Aurora got it wrong, she wanted to say. But really, she hadn't. She'd seen her mother's offhand, snippy manner with Jamie whenever they met – until recently, at least. What was Aurora meant to think? She only hoped the children hadn't picked up her snobbery too. 'Of course I'll apologise to Jamie. Maybe I can catch him before school finishes.'

'Probably best to let him get on with things for a bit,' said Alf. 'He's got a lot on his plate at the moment. Maybe a quick apology if you happen to see him, then leave it for a day or two. Or when he comes in next. Oh, and, er...'

'Yes?' Saffron stood poised.

'You might want to go in the back and wash your face.' Alf looked bashful. 'I hate to say it, but you're a bit, um...'

Janet nodded vigorously. 'I didn't like to mention, but you look a right state.'

Saffron grimaced at her reflection in the bathroom mirror. Her supposedly waterproof mascara was streaked down her cheeks and her nose and eyes were red from crying. Gently, she washed away the black trails and regarded herself in the mirror. Normally, she would grab her make-up bag and repair the damage by slapping on another layer, but now it didn't matter. Her priority was to do whatever it would take to put things right.

10

Saffron walked along the road to school, dreading what was to come.

When she had finally checked her phone, an hour before pickup time, she found a voicemail from school. 'Hello, this is Mrs Hanratty, Roar's teacher. Please could you come to pickup fifteen minutes early. I'd like a word.'

A pause. Saffron hoped she was about to say 'You're not in trouble.'

'Please can you let the office know whether you can make it. Thank you.'

Saffron deleted the message, then rang school to say that she would be there. 'Thank you,' sing-songed whoever was on reception. *Glad you're so pleased*, thought Saffron. *At least it isn't the headteacher. Yet.*

She reached the gate, let herself in and walked round to the junior playground. Thankfully, Jamie wasn't on patrol. *I can't face him, not yet. And I have to talk to Aurora and Chad first.*

The classroom windows were covered with tinted film, but she could just see heads bent over pieces of paper. She was about to tap on the window when Mrs Hanratty opened the door. 'Ten minutes left, class,' she said. 'Ask Mrs Luckhurst if you need more paper.' She let the door fall to, then walked to a bench a short distance away. Saffron followed.

'I'm so sorry about this morning,' said Saffron. 'If I'd known you were coming…'

'I wish you'd said something beforehand,' said Mrs Hanratty. 'Either to Roar, or to me.'

'I suppose they've been talking about it all day.' Saffron looked at her feet.

'What they have been talking about is you doing a runner. None of them understand, because they think working in a shop where there are sweets and crisps and fizzy drinks is a cool job. Whatever you may think of it.'

'It's – it's a nice job. I enjoy it. But it's not what I saw myself doing.'

'When I was a kid, I wanted to be lead singer in a band.' Mrs Hanratty leaned back on the bench. 'I practised in front of the mirror until I drove my family round the bend. I did GCSE music, then A-level, and auditioned for loads of local groups. Unfortunately, they didn't want a short, plump lead singer. I tried forming my own, but I couldn't get that off the ground either. And no, that wasn't fair. So instead, I run a choir and I'm the school's subject lead for music. It's not my dream, but I still get to do what I love and help other people enjoy it too.'

'I'm sorry,' said Saffron.

'I'm not,' said Mrs Hanratty. 'Not now. I can't imagine myself on a tour bus, and my kids would miss me.' For a moment, she looked a bit misty-eyed. 'Anyway, I told Roar earlier that you'd phoned and you were OK.'

'Is she OK?' *That should have been the first thing I asked.* She wanted to smack her own forehead.

Mrs Hanratty smiled. 'She was worried about you. I don't think she minds you working in a shop at all. She was just puzzled as to why you hadn't told her. You will explain to her, I take it?'

'Yes, of course.'

'Good. She's said sorry to Mr Sullivan. Not that that was really her fault.'

'I'll be apologising to him too,' said Saffron. She sighed. 'I have a lot of climbing down to do.'

'Don't be too hard on yourself,' said Mrs Hanratty. 'People will understand.' She stood up. 'I'd better go and put them out of their misery. Nothing like a surprise test to take their mind off things.'

People were drifting into the playground. Some waved to Saffron, and she waved back. *Would they be waving if they knew?* Then she shrugged. *If they don't want to talk to me because I work in a shop, it's their loss.*

The bell rang. Saffron faced the classroom door.

***

'So does that mean we get free stuff?' asked Chad, for the third time.

'Not all the time,' said Saffron. 'It's a perk of the job. And no, that doesn't include sweets.' She sighed. 'I should have told you at the start. That would have been the sensible thing to do, but even grown-ups aren't always sensible.'

'We know that, Mummy,' said Aurora. 'Our teachers are silly sometimes. Like when they wear costumes for World Book Day or play pranks on each other.'

'Yes, but that's fun silly,' said Saffron. 'Not silly silly, which is what I was. I didn't lie, exactly, but I didn't tell you the whole truth. I was embarrassed that we needed the money. But the price of everything is rising, so I had to do something, and this came along, and—'

'It's all right, Mummy,' said Aurora. She got down from the breakfast bar, came round to Saffron and reached up for a hug.

'If anyone's ever mean to you because of it, tell me. Or your teacher.' Mrs Hanratty would sort the kids out far more effectively than she could, she thought wryly. *So much for those communication seminars.*

'They won't be. Everyone wants to know whether you get to push the buttons on the big cash register and put prices on things with one of those sticker guns.'

Saffron laughed. 'Yes. Yes, I do. Maybe, if it fits in with what you're learning, you could visit the shop again and we could show you.'

'Wow,' breathed Aurora.

'Mum...' said Chad.

'Yes?' Saffron said warily. *I've been so busy making sure Aurora's all right. Have I neglected Chad? He's not traumatised, is he?*

'What's for tea?'

She wasn't sure whether she wanted to laugh or cry most. 'I don't know. To be honest, I haven't thought.' She looked in the fridge, then the cupboard. 'How about . . . risotto?'

'With cheese on top?'

'Yes, with cheese on top.'

He grinned and gave her a thumbs up.

***

Saffron woke early the next morning. As she was doing her morning yoga, she pondered the contents of her wardrobe. *Boden? Whistles? White Stuff?*

What's the point? You may as well save those for going out.

Yes, but... I'll feel better if I can hide behind my glam mum uniform.

Which you've been doing far too long. You're still you, whatever you wear.

So Saffron put on one of her shop tops and her black wide-leg trousers. She put her hair up, and restricted herself to tinted moisturiser and one coat of mascara. *He's seen me in shop clothes loads of times*, she thought, as she filled the toaster. *He won't care what I'm wearing.* She blinked, pressed her lips together and got the butter and jam from the fridge.

She walked the children to school with her head held high, ready to be ignored, ostracised and whispered about. However, as far as she could tell, everyone was busy getting their children to school on time and with all their belongings. *You idiot. Thinking you'd be the centre of attention.*

In the playground, the same people as usual said hello. Then she felt a tap on her shoulder and turned.

'Hello there,' said Heather, with a wry smile. 'I believe word's got out.'

'It has,' said Saffron. 'Which is OK.'

'Good.' Heather looked relieved.

'Thank you for recommending me in the first place. I'm not sure I thanked you at the time, but I've learnt a lot.'

'About running a shop?'

'And other things too.'

Someone vaguely familiar was heading over. As she moved closer, Saffron recognised Becca.

'Hi,' Becca said, shifting from foot to foot, and Saffron wondered what was coming next. 'Ellie says one of her classmates told her her sister said you were working at the Country Stores.'

The grapevine's in full working order. 'Yes, that's right,' said Saffron, trying not to sound abrupt.

'I came to say that . . . if you ever want to talk shops, we could maybe swap ideas?' She was so timid and hesitant that Saffron could have hugged her.

'That would be great,' she said. 'There's a lot you can teach me.'

Becca's eyes widened and she beamed. 'I'll send you a text.'

The bell rang, and Saffron watched the lines of children file into classrooms as their parents drifted towards their destiny for the day. She sighed. *Time to face Jamie.*

11

Saffron walked slower and slower as she neared the school entrance. The door was locked, so she pressed the door buzzer. 'Yes?' the intercom crackled.

'It's Saffron. Saffron Montgomery.'

'How can I help?' The voice sounded like Angie. Saffron had the distinct impression that Angie wasn't keen on her, though she wasn't sure why. *Probably my fault.*

She brushed that aside for the moment. 'I wondered if I could speak to J— To Mr Sullivan. The caretaker.'

'One moment.' A phone was ringing in the background. The intercom went dead for a couple of minutes, then came back to life. 'Sorry about that,' Angie said perkily. 'What was it you wanted?'

'Can I speak to Mr Sullivan, if he's available.'

'Ah. Sorry, he isn't in today.'

'Not in?'

'No, he has a day off,' Angie said, as if explaining to a child.

'Oh.' Saffron became conscious of a heavy feeling in her chest. *It's Friday. I can't hang on to this all weekend.* 'It's just that – it's important.'

'May I ask what it's concerning?'

A number of replies to Angie's question flashed through Saffron's mind, none appropriate in a school setting. 'It's... It's not a school matter.'

'Ohhhhhh.' While Saffron couldn't see Angie through the glass door, she was pretty sure she was grinning like the Cheshire Cat. 'Actually, he *did* leave a message . . . where is it, now...'

Saffron's heart thumped. What would the message be? She imagined the intercom crackling into life and Angie reading out: *You are the rudest, most ungrateful person I've ever met*, or *Please don't talk to me ever again*, or *I'm taking my business to another shop.*

'Here we are,' said Angie. 'He said, "If anyone comes looking for me today on a non-school matter, I'm at the Icon gallery in Meadborough this morning." There you go, Ms Montgomery. Have a good day.' The intercom went dead.

Saffron checked her watch. If she hurried home and got straight in the car, she could make it to Meadborough and back and not be late for work.

Thank heavens I didn't put those stupid boots on, she thought, as she ran.

***

By some kind of miracle, the traffic was light. Saffron was in Meadborough and parked by twenty-five past nine. The Icon Gallery, where she had bought a couple of paintings and now visited just to look, was a short walk away. She got an hour's free ticket and ran.

She had been so focused on getting to the gallery that she hadn't given any thought to why Jamie was there. Did he do painting and decorating on the side? That would explain the state of his clothes. Being a caretaker couldn't pay much, so she didn't blame him.

The door of the gallery was open, but the windows were covered with dust sheets. *Yup, redecorating.* A piece of paper was stuck in the middle of the window. *That'll be to say when they reopen*, she thought, glancing at it.

OPENING TOMORROW
RURAL ROMANCE:
PAINTINGS BY JAMIE SULLIVAN

Her eyes widened. *But—*

The paint-stained jeans. Driving to the middle of nowhere every lunch break. Alf's caginess about what Jamie might be doing.

And you never worked it out, because the school caretaker couldn't possibly be a painter. She thought of what Mrs Hanratty had told her the day before. Then she recalled the end of year concerts, the school orchestra, the school music competition, and her face flamed. *I'll say my piece and go.*

The gallery was cool and seemed empty. The lights were on, though, and a few paintings were already hung. Saffron's feet took her towards them.

There was the Country Stores, its lights on, a little beacon in a rolling landscape of dark fields and hills. A huge farm machine loomed among wildflowers. A woman roamed in a field of corn. She had long brown hair with blonde highlights, and wore a striped top and jeans…

She heard voices, and Dan the gallery owner entered from the back. 'Oh, hello, um…'

'Saffron Montgomery. I've bought from you before.'

'Oh yes, of course. I'm afraid we aren't actually open—'

Jamie appeared in the doorway. 'It's OK, Dan. Would you mind if I took a quick break?' He was wearing his usual scruffy jeans and T-shirt. She couldn't tell what he was thinking.

Dan raised his eyebrows. 'Someone from the local paper's coming at ten to ten.'

'So we've got a few minutes.'

'Sure,' said Dan, and strode off, shoulders tense.

Jamie walked to the furthest corner of the shop and Saffron followed. 'I assume you've come out here for a reason,' he said, his face still neutral.

'I'm so sorry about what happened yesterday,' she said. 'I don't hate you or dislike you, not at all. I used to, and it was stupid of me, but now I know better. Thank you for helping, even though it was my own fault.'

'Uh-huh.' He stood, looking at her. 'Apology accepted,' he said, and smiled.

'It wasn't Aurora's fault,' she said. 'It was mine. Please don't be hard on her.'

'Wouldn't dream of it. Kids make mistakes all the time.'

'Not just kids. I really am sorry. If there's anything I can do…'

'Half price on everything in the shop?' He grinned.

Saffron returned the grin. 'That's for Alf and Janet to decide.' She glanced about her. 'I hadn't realised you were a painter. An artist, I mean.'

'It's not something that comes up when I'm telling you off for parking where you shouldn't,' he said. 'When I took the caretaker job a few years back, I decided to keep the art stuff out of it. I didn't want to be one of those people who talk up their side hustle and neglect their job. Although it does sneak in.'

'How?'

'Well, I run an art club, and sometimes Mrs Patterson, the subject lead, asks me to help with the older kids. She's part-time, so it means the kids don't miss out. I was working with your lad the other day. Chad, is it? He's pretty good.'

Saffron recalled her attempts at school conversation with Chad. *Dunno. Something after lunch.* 'Which I'd know if he ever talked about school.'

Jamie grinned. 'Not just your kids.'

A cough came from the other side of the gallery. 'I think Dan's trying to drop a hint,' said Jamie. 'And you've got a shop to run.'

Saffron glanced at her watch. 'Oh heck, yes I have.'

Jamie took a flyer from a nearby table and gave it to her. 'If you fancy it, we open tomorrow. Bring the kids, if you want. Tell them I said hi.'

'I will.' She waited for him to say goodbye, to move off, but he didn't. 'That picture, of the woman in the cornfield… She looks like me.'

He bit his lip. 'She does a bit, doesn't she?'

She smiled. 'Since you're an art megastar, I assume you'll be wined and dined for lunch today?'

He laughed. 'Nah. I'll be here this morning, then coming to the shop for my usual.'

'In that case, I'll save you a BLT. I really must go. Catch you later.' She made to pat his shoulder in farewell, but he moved and she touched his arm, warm and muscular. A tingle spread right through her.

She hurried to the car, feeling as if she must be glowing like a lightbulb. She was still holding the flyer. She tried to shove it in her bag, but something was in the way. *What's in there?* She put her hand in and her fingers brushed cardboard. She pulled out the scratch card Jamie had given her and stared at it, then grinned. *Why not?*

She got in the car, found a coin in the cupholder and rubbed. *No . . . no . . . no— Wait...*

Saffron stared at the little piece of card, unable to believe what she was seeing. She took a couple of deep breaths, pulled her phone from her bag and dialled.

12

'Roar! Chad! Time for breakfast!' Saffron paused, for effect. 'Otherwise I'll have to eat all these pancakes myself.'

A few seconds later, two doors slammed upstairs and the children came clattering down. 'Cheers, Mum,' said Chad, as he jogged past.

'Don't mention it.' She'd known that pancakes would get them out of bed. She definitely didn't want them being late on the first day of the new school year.

'I can't believe I'm in year six,' said Roar. 'Top of the school.'

'Yes, and you'll have to set an example,' said Saffron. 'Being as you're deputy head girl.'

Roar grimaced. 'Don't remind me.'

'You'll be fine.' Saffron reached over and ruffled her hair. 'Now eat up.' She took a pancake for herself and added sugar, lemon and banana slices.

'Are you at the shop today, Mum?' asked Chad.

'I am in the morning. In the afternoon, Alf and I are speaking to a group of local business owners about community outreach and reducing food waste.'

'Wow,' said Roar. 'That's cool.'

Saffron smiled. 'I suppose it is.'

Once everyone was ready, Saffron led the way past Taylor, the small red electric car on the drive, and they set off for school. The children surged ahead, calling to friends and running to catch them.

Saffron strolled, enjoying the slight chill in the air, welcome after a baking summer. Doing the school run seemed a bit pointless now that the children were perfectly capable of going on their own, but she wasn't ready to give it up yet. And of course, there was Jamie.

Today he was mending the fence, wrapping tape round some broken wires.

'Morning,' she called.

He gave her a cheeky grin. 'Good morning yourself.' He held her gaze until the mass of parents and children squeezing by threatened to send her flying.

'I'd better go,' she said, giggling, and allowed the stream to carry her along. *He'll be in later, anyway.*

She went to the junior playground and checked the children were where they should be and still in possession of their school bags, then kissed them both and stood back. Chad slouched as usual, but Roar stood tall. *Don't worry too much about the responsibility, Roar*, thought Saffron. *Don't forget to have fun.*

As she left, she waved to a few people she knew, including Becca. They had met for a quick chat at the end of the summer term, half an hour before school pickup, and done some video chats over the holidays. *One day I'll be able to go out in the evenings and see friends.* Then she thought of the weekend to come and smiled. *Got to earn the pennies first.* She walked home, got into Taylor, and drove the nippy little car to the Country Stores.

'Howdy, partner,' said Alf, who was sitting at the counter pricing tins.

'Howdy,' said Saffron, with a grin.

***

The first thing she had done after playing the scratch card was to phone the shop. 'Something odd's happened, Alf,' she said. 'It's good, but I'll be a bit late. I'll tell you when I get in.'

Saffron walked to the gallery. Through the glass panel in the door she could see Tim, the nice reporter from the *Meadborough and District Times*, talking to Dan. Jamie stood near, arms folded. She opened the door and went in.

Jamie gave her a quizzical look. 'Shouldn't you be

at work?' he whispered.

Saffron handed him the scratch card. He glanced at it, his eyebrows shot up, and he whistled.

Dan and Tim glanced round. *Sorry*, he mouthed.

He took Saffron to the other end of the room and handed back the scratch card. 'You've got that luck you needed, then,' he murmured.

'I can't take it,' Saffron whispered. 'It's yours.'

'I gave it to you.'

'What are we going to do? Are you really telling me that you don't want the money?'

He shrugged. 'It isn't mine.'

'How about we split it?'

Jamie considered this. 'OK,' he said, eventually. 'If you change your mind, that's all right. You've got kids to worry about.'

'Half each,' said Saffron, and stuck out her hand.

'You're on,' Jamie said, and shook it.

It wasn't life-changing money, not for either of them. But it was enough to make things considerably more secure. Saffron put some away for the children, some into savings, and treated herself to a couple of luxuries. With the rest, she bought a share in the Country Stores. And she carried on working there.

***

As usual, the morning flew. Now that Jeff's marrow had won first prize at the county show, he was considering what giant autumnal veg he could grow. Several people had harvested more apples than they knew what to do with, and wanted Saffron's help to use them before they went bad. On top of that, the trolley for moving heavy goods had a loose wheel which needed attention.

Saffron was wiping her hands on a cloth when Jamie walked in. 'Got any sarnies left?'

'We're down to egg and cress.' She laughed at his disappointed face. 'There's a tomato, mozzarella and basil one hiding in the corner.'

'Lovely.' He walked over and claimed it, with a packet of ready-salted crisps and a bottle of 7-Up. 'Still on for Saturday?'

'Oh yes.' Saffron went to the counter and rang up the purchases.

The children had been annoyed that they would miss out on a day trip. 'Why does Dad have to have us this weekend?' grumbled Chad.

'Don't be silly,' said Saffron, 'you'll have a great time. Aren't you going to that Minions movie?'

'Oh yeah,' said Chad. 'S'pose.'

Jamie was taking her to Meadingley Magna, a little village about twenty miles away. Weather permitting, they would stroll, scout for new painting subjects, and have a picnic. There might even be scope for a lunchtime drink at the village pub.

'Would you mind if I took sketching gear?' asked Jamie. 'Not to draw for hours, just to get some impressions.'

'Fine by me,' said Saffron. 'I'll bring a book.'

The corners of his mouth curled up in a way she found hard to resist. 'Would you mind if I sketched you?'

'I'll have to think about that.'

Saffron imagined herself in a gallery, or on someone's wall. It would be Jamie's achievement, not hers, but she didn't mind at all.

The Secret Santa

1

It's just a meeting, Becca told herself as she walked into the village. *It'll be fine.*

It's the last committee meeting before the Meadley Christmas Festival on Saturday week. Anyone could ask me anything.

If only – but no, that wasn't fair. Declan had a ton of paperwork to do, and it wasn't as if he needed to be there. For any primary-school matters, the PTA head, Saffron, was more than capable of reporting back. 'And if I get that headteacher's report done tonight,' he had said, with the smile which always won Becca over, 'it means I'm free another time. When you are, too.'

'OK, OK.' Becca gazed at him. 'Promise me nothing bad will happen.'

'What could possibly happen at a committee meeting?' said Declan. 'That's the problem with them – generally nothing *does* happen. Although, to be fair, the festival committee do actually get things done. I mean, they've got you on board with an exciting new initiative from the charity bookshop.'

'Don't remind me,' muttered Becca.

I don't even have Ellie as an excuse, she thought, as she dug her hands further into her coat pockets and watched her breath become smoke. Ellie was sleeping over at her dad's, and while Becca was very glad that Phil was finally acting like a parent, it couldn't have come at a worse time.

Nothing bad will happen, she told herself firmly, and hurried towards the community centre.

***

'Good grief, the time!' Julie sprang up from the table and went in search of her coat.

'Oh yes,' said Neil, 'it's your thingy meeting, isn't it.'

'Festival committee. I'd better get moving, or I'll be late.' Her stomach grumbled faintly in protest.

'You can't still be hungry,' said Neil, looking at her empty bowl.

'It isn't that,' said Julie. 'The jambalaya was a bit more . . . spicy than I anticipated.'

'I only put in two chillies,' said Neil.

Julie's eyes narrowed. 'Big ones or little ones?'

Neil considered. 'Sort of medium,' he said, eventually.

Julie went to the fridge, poured herself a glass of milk and took a long draught. 'It's probably nerves.'

'What have you got to be nervous about? Your monster Christmas crochet project is going great, and your group has loads of things for the craft stall.'

Julie sighed. 'I suppose I want everything to be perfect.' She let out a tiny burp and clapped her hand to her mouth.

Neil grinned. 'Nobody's perfect. See you later!'

***

Saffron hopped around the hall, tugging on her right boot. 'Do you all remember what I've asked you to do?'

'Yes,' they chorused from the dining room.

'Prove it,' she called back.

'I'm scraping the plates,' said Chad.

'I'm loading the dishwasher,' said Roar.

'I'm watching *Pulp Fiction* with the kids,' said Jamie.

Saffron was at the doorway in two seconds. Jamie held up his hands. 'OK, that was a joke. I'll make sure the kids don't kill each other and get them to bed at a reasonable time.'

'That's the one,' she said. 'In return for the lovely meal I've cooked you.'

'It absolutely was.' Jamie stuck his legs out under the table and rested his hands on his stomach. 'Now, you've organised us. Go and organise everyone at the meeting.'

'Sir yes sir!' Saffron saluted and the children giggled.

'And don't go taking on anything else,' added Jamie.

'You can talk, high-flying artist and school caretaker.'

'That's different,' said Jamie. 'I know you. If there aren't any extra responsibilities for you to shoulder, you'll probably invent some. You're the one who proposed making recipe cards to go with Alf's Tin-Can Tombola. Not to mention the festival soup kitchen.'

'Soup's easy,' said Saffron. 'The recipes only needed typing up and printing.'

'And photos, and layout,' said Jamie. 'Maybe I should add food photographer to my CV.'

'Maybe you should.' Suddenly, she frowned and sniffed the air. 'I forgot the cookies!' She dashed into the kitchen, opened the oven door and flapped away the smoke. 'It's all right,' she called. 'They're just a bit caramelised on top.'

'They'll be fine,' said Jamie. 'Don't forget to leave us s—'

'Lip gloss!' Saffron exclaimed. 'I knew there was something!' And she ran upstairs as Jamie, Roar and Chad grinned at each other.

2

'Let's begin,' said Paul from the Lions, surveying the group. 'Who's chairing?'

Everyone looked elsewhere.

'Come on,' said Paul. 'I'd do it, but I missed the last meeting so I'm not really up to speed. Saffron's missing, and so is Declan.'

Becca studied the table so hard that she could have drawn the wood veneer from memory. Then someone coughed, and she couldn't help glancing up.

'Ah, Becca, would you mind?' said Paul. 'You always seem on top of things, and I'm sure you can control this rabble if they get rowdy.'

'Go on, Becca,' said Mrs Walentynowicz. 'Let's get this party started, or we'll be here all night.'

Becca swallowed. 'Um . . . well... OK.' She studied the agenda. 'Umm . . . is everyone happy with the minutes of the last meeting?'

Various nods and expressions of agreement came from round the table.

'Right, um, good. We'll go to item two, updates. I'll do mine first, then we'll go clockwise round the table.' Charlotte, the clerk of the parish council who acted as the committee's secretary, smiled encouragingly at her.

Fifteen minutes later, it had been established that the festival was well within budget, due to several generous donations from the local community. Becca's book-donation drive had attracted lots of new stock, and her mystery book lucky dip was almost ready. Denise, owner of Café de Paris in the village centre, had confirmed that mince pies and mulled wine, plus vegan and non-alcoholic versions, would be available. Mrs Walentynowicz had recruited ten helpers to dress the village with festive garlands and provide a wreath for every front door in the village centre. Julie had reported that the Hooked On Yarn craft group were on course to complete their Christmas postbox topper.

'Go on, tell us what it is,' wheedled Mrs Walentynowicz.

Julie's stomach growled and she looked rather nervous. 'I could,' she said, 'but Tegan would kill me. She's had sleepless nights with this one. Anyway, it will be worth it, I promise. You'll just have to wait and see.' She laughed at their groans and grumbles.

'And we have more than enough items for the craft stall.'

'Sorry I'm late,' called Saffron, hurrying into the hall bearing a tray covered with a tea towel. 'Cookie-related incident.'

'A good one, I hope,' said Paul. 'It smells very tempting.'

Saffron came to the table, set down the tray and whipped off the towel. 'I'm calling these triple C cookies. Carrot, currant and cinnamon.' The agenda was forgotten for a minute or two while everyone helped themselves. 'Did I miss much?'

'We're doing updates,' said Becca. 'All good so far.'

'Excellent,' said Saffron. 'My update is that we have two hundred tins for the Tin-Can Tombola, if needed, with accompanying recipe cards. Also, my kids have taste-tested and approved five different soups, made with veg donated by local farmers and shops.'

'Wonderful,' said Becca. She watched Charlotte's pen until it stopped. 'Anything else to add?'

'Oh yes, the road closure for the float and the carols is sorted,' said Charlotte. She glanced to her left. 'Paul, all OK with the Santa float?'

'We've organised the flatbed, got Santa's sleigh out of hibernation and tested the fairy lights. I'll just check in with Barry and confirm he's on board.'

Becca raised her eyebrows. 'Barry?'

'Barry's always Santa on the Christmas float,' said Saffron. 'At least, as far back as I can remember.'

Paul leaned to his left and retrieved his mobile from his trouser pocket. 'I'll text him now.' He tapped at the screen with his forefinger.

'So, to confirm the festival timings,' said Charlotte. 'The road through the village closes at quarter to one. At one o'clock, Santa's float progresses slowly through the outskirts of the village, travelling by the agreed route. At one thirty the mysterious Christmas postbox topper is revealed, the community centre opens and the festival begins. At two, Santa arrives at the community centre. At four, the community centre closes and everyone gathers for carols round the village Christmas tree. Agreed?'

'Agreed,' everyone chorused.

Paul's phone beeped and all eyes were on him. He touched the screen and his face fell.

'What is it?' said Becca.

'It's a message from Barry and it's not good news, I'm afraid. I'll read it out.' He held the phone a bit further away. '"Hi Paul and thanks for your message. Unfortunately I've got the flu so I can't be Santa this year. Happy to lend suit and beard to my replacement. If anything changes, I'll let you know."' He looked around the table. 'Anyone fancy being Santa? I can't, because I'll be driving the float.'

A table of women gazed at him.

'Um... I could ask at Lions,' he said. 'Although most of our members will be on the streets with buckets, collecting for charity. Even if they weren't, those are big boots to fill. Barry *is* Santa.'

'Don't worry,' said Saffron, firmly. 'We'll come up with something between us. I'm sure we can find a willing volunteer somewhere in Meadley. The village won't let us down.'

'I'm sure it won't,' said Becca, wondering how Declan was getting on with his report, and what sort of mood he might be in.

3

The committee members lingered in the community centre, saying their goodbyes and chatting. 'Anyone fancy a quick drink?' said Paul.

'Not for me,' said Becca. 'School night.' Technically it wasn't, since Phil would be taking care of Ellie and school in the morning, but she'd still have to get up for work. Besides, she had more important things to do...

Once she was clear of the community centre, she took out her phone and began typing. *How's the report going?*

Slowly, came Declan's reply, thirty seconds later.

Becca snorted. Ten to one he was blasting rock music and wondering why he found it hard to concentrate. *Would you be able to lend a hand with something?*

Depends what it is. Is it more interesting than this

report?

Definitely. She sent the message and waited.

Well go on then!

How would you like to be Santa?

The next reply took considerably longer to come. *Doesn't Barry usually do that?*

He's got flu.

Oh. Three dots wibbled up and down. This continued for some time. *Is he writing me an essay?*

I'll have Jack and Sophie next weekend. Also, it's very likely at least one of the kids from school will spot me. It'll mess with their heads if they start thinking Santa Claus is their headteacher. What would that do to discipline?

Doesn't Santa tell kids they have to be good? Becca replied, but in her heart she knew the battle was lost. *Thanks anyway*, she added, and put her phone away.

I can't believe I forgot he has the kids next weekend, she thought as she trudged along the road. *Maybe I should have gone for a drink after all.*

***

Julie knocked on Neil's door.

'You're back early,' he said, when he opened it. 'Fancy a brew?'

'Oh yes.' Julie stepped inside and unwound her scarf.

'All OK?' said Neil, from the kitchen.

'Mostly.'

Neil looked over his shoulder at her. 'How so? Stallholders fighting for the best pitch? Christmas cracker wars?'

'Very funny. We have a Santa problem. The guy who normally does it has the flu.'

'Ah.' He opened the mug cupboard.

'I don't suppose…' His shoulders stiffened. *In for a penny…* 'I don't suppose you fancy being Santa? It's only for the afternoon, on Saturday week.'

Neil's frame relaxed. 'I'm afraid I'm busy. It's the Christmas meeting of the nature reserve trustees that afternoon, followed by drinks.'

'Oh.'

'And frankly, it isn't really my thing. Can you see me going "Ho ho ho" and being jolly for a whole afternoon? I don't have it in me.'

'I'm sure you could if you tried,' said Julie. She sighed. 'Sorry. I didn't think it would be your cup of tea, but I thought I might as well ask.'

'Hey, it's OK.' Neil came over and gave her a hug. 'Speaking of cups of tea, I'll get the kettle on.'

***

'I'm home!' called Saffron.

She followed the noise of the TV and found Jamie and the children laughing at *Monsters Inc*.

Jamie turned his head. 'There's about twenty minutes left,' he said. 'They'll be a bit late to bed, but not much.'

'May I borrow you for a minute?' Saffron moved her head slightly in the direction of the kitchen.

Jamie heaved himself up from the sofa. 'You can borrow me for five if you want.' He followed her to the kitchen. Saffron sat at the breakfast bar and he followed suit. 'What's up? I checked with the kids and they said they'd watched the film before and you wouldn't mind.'

'No, that's fine.' She leaned towards him. 'I have a job for you.'

'Oh yes? What might that be?'

'Santa at the Christmas festival.'

Jamie burst out laughing. 'Me?'

'Shhh! They'll hear you.'

'I'm a bit young. Maybe in thirty years…'

'Go on, you'll enjoy it. It's Saturday week, in the afternoon.'

'Ah. The thing is, I've got tickets for the football and kick off's at three. It's a local derby, and the teams are very close. It could make a big difference to our chances in the league.' His face lit up. 'I know, why don't you be Santa? You like volunteering for things, and… Equal opportunities, and all that. You can be Mama Claus!'

'I will, if I have to,' said Saffron. 'But if I do, you'll be on the naughty list.'

4

Despite – or perhaps because of – their failures on the Santa front, Becca, Julie and Saffron redoubled their efforts to make their own parts of Meadley Christmas Festival a success. Becca spent every evening gift-wrapping books with Ellie. Julie checked in with Tegan and the other members of Hooked On Yarn twice a day on average, and her festival spreadsheet was constantly open. Meanwhile, Saffron fine-tuned her soups and put together a hamper to raffle off.

She also texted Paul from the Lions. *Any news on Santa? Hoping you'll tell me Barry's made a miraculous recovery.*

Paul's reply didn't come until that evening. *Sorry, only just saw this. Barry's still on the sick list, I'm afraid, but someone's stepped up to be Santa, so all's well that ends well. See you Saturday!*

'They got a Santa,' she told Jamie, who was sitting

at the breakfast bar road-testing the latest version of spiced butternut squash soup.

'Oh good.'

'So you needn't feel guilty any more.'

He grinned. 'I wasn't. I'd make a terrible Santa and you know it.'

'You're used to kids.'

'Yeah, but as a caretaker and when I'm doing art club. It's not quite the same.'

'S'pose.' She reached over and ruffled his hair.

'Oi!' He smoothed it. 'You'd never dare do that to the real Santa. I just don't have the gravitas.'

***

Julie set a basket of crocheted Christmas baubles in the middle of the stall. 'Do you think we've got enough?'

Natalie laughed. 'Everyone in the village could buy something and we'd still have stuff left. When I close my eyes at night, I see snowmen.'

Julie stepped back and regarded the table critically. 'OK, fair point.' She checked her watch. 'They're unveiling the topper in two minutes! But the stall…'

'Don't worry, I'll mind it for you,' said Charlotte.

'Thanks!' And the members of Hooked On Yarn set off at a jog.

When they reached the post office, a crowd was already gathered and staring at the postbox, which was currently covered with a black cloth. It was also three feet taller than usual.

'What do you think it will be?' asked a woman in front of Julie.

'Knowing that lot, it could be anything,' her neighbour replied.

I hope they like it... Julie stood on tiptoe and looked for Tegan. There she was, by the window of the post office, appearing as nervous as Julie felt. Julie realised she was digging her nails into her palms and hastily unclenched her fists.

The head of the parish council, Nigel, stepped forward. 'Hello everyone, nice day for it!'

The crowd rumbled their assent.

'Now, I could make a speech about team effort and pulling together and all that, but I'm sure you'd rather get your mitts on a mince pie and say hello to Santa. So, with thanks to Hooked On Yarn and, er, Feminist Death Knits, I'll unveil their handiwork and declare Meadley Christmas Festival officially open!' He pulled off the black cloth. 'Good heavens.'

The postbox was topped with a snowy hill, wound with holly and mistletoe. Bunches of snowdrops poked out here and there. Round the bottom of the topper was a knitted fence, on which perched a bevy of robins, and on the top of the hill sat a smiling snowman.

The crowd oohed and aahed.

Tegan walked to the back of the postbox and Julie

crossed her fingers.

'The First Nowell' began to play.

'What the— It's coming from the postbox!'

'Look, the snowman's swaying from side to side! He's dancing to the music.'

'The robins are too!'

'Wow, cool!'

The crowd broke into applause. There were whistles too, and a couple of cheers. Tegan punched the air, grinning.

'How do they come up with this stuff?' said the woman in front of Julie.

Julie closed her eyes, heaved a gentle sigh of relief and pulled out her phone. *Topper unveiled successfully*, she texted.

Good stuff, Neil replied. *Told you solar with a normal battery as backup would work. You can relax now.*

Julie laughed. Then she saw people heading for the community centre and broke into a run.

***

Saffron was ladling carrot and coriander soup into cups when the walkie-talkie at her hip crackled and a faint voice said 'Do you copy?' Whatever that meant.

'Roar, can you look after these customers?'

'Sure,' said Roar, and stepped forward. 'Can I interest you in a raffle ticket for our hamper?'

Good girl, thought Saffron, as she unclipped the

walkie-talkie. 'Sorry, I was serving,' she said. 'Um, over.'

'Two-minute warning for Santa, over,' said Paul. 'Repeat, two-minute warning for Santa.'

'Message received, over and out.' Saffron put down the walkie-talkie and clapped her hands. No one paid any attention. 'Santa's on his way!' she shouted, and everyone turned round. 'He'll be here very soon.'

There was a scramble for the door. In less than a minute, the community centre was empty apart from the stallholders.

'Let's go and see Santa arrive, Mummy,' said Roar.

'Yes, why not.' Saffron wiped her hands on her apron and walked outside with the children.

A special parking space had been designated for Santa by the door. 'We'll have a great view,' said Roar.

'He's coming!' someone cried. 'Here's the float!'

Santa's float approached at a dignified pace, playing Christmas music and twinkling with lights. Saffron could just make out Paul at the wheel. She gave him a thumbs up, but his gaze was fixed on the road. At last the float eased into the parking space.

'Ho ho ho!' boomed Santa, who was sitting on a throne apparently made of presents and flanked by two elves who were normally teaching assistants at the primary school.

'Hello, Santa!' shouted all the children and some

of the adults.

'Hello, everyone!' He certainly looked the part: Santa suit and hat, curly white wig, bushy white beard and round wire-rimmed glasses. But Saffron noted that Santa's beard was so full and his hat was pulled so low that only eyes, nose and pink cheeks were visible. And rather than descending from the float in the normal ponderous manner, he bounded down the steps, large tummy notwithstanding.

The crowd parted to let Santa and the elves enter the community centre, where a grotto was set up for them in the corner with chairs for Santa, the elves and the visiting child.

Saffron went over to Paul, who was dismounting from the cab. 'Mission accomplished for another year,' he said. 'Well, it will be once I've de-Christmased the flatbed and dropped it off.'

Saffron leaned closer. 'So who *is* Santa?' she murmured.

'Friend of a friend,' said Paul. 'I don't know him personally. He seems to be doing a good job.'

'Yes,' said Saffron. 'I'd better get back in there.'

'Indeed, yes,' said Paul. 'Got any soup left?'

'Vats of the stuff. Come and take your pick.' But as a queue of children formed at the grotto, Saffron resolved that however busy it got, she'd find time to take a closer look at Santa.

5

The community centre was full of people moving from one stall to another, or waiting in line with their children to meet Santa.

Julie was kept busy by people who had questions about the postbox topper, or the three-for-two offer on Christmas baubles, but every so often she found herself idly gazing at Santa's grotto. Not that there was much to see: a line of children and parents snaked patiently around the area, and all she could make out was the top of Santa's hat.

Saffron's stall was also busy. Janet from the Country Stores had come to assist with the Tin-Can Tombola, and Roar and Chad were sort of helping, but Saffron was everywhere at once, serving soup, selling raffle tickets and offering people recipe cards to go with their tin cans. Yet she also glanced towards Santa's grotto every so often.

'Can you hold the fort for a minute?' Julie asked Bernie and Natalie.

'Course,' said Natalie, pushing a strand of hair out of her eyes.

Julie walked across to the soup kitchen. 'Hello, what soup would you like?' said Saffron, on automatic pilot. 'Oh sorry, hi, Julie.'

'This looks great,' said Julie. 'But I came over because I saw you eyeballing Santa.'

'Oh heck, is it that obvious?' Saffron rolled her eyes.

'Is something wrong?'

'No, nothing like that. It's just... I'm wondering who Santa is. Obviously it's not Barry, and he seems unusually sprightly for a gentleman of his advanced age.'

'Mmm,' said Julie. 'I noticed that.'

'I'm dying to get a closer look, but it's been too busy,' muttered Saffron.

'I could wander over,' said Julie. 'We've got a few people on the stall and it's less complicated than yours.'

'Fab,' said Saffron. 'Let me know how it goes.'

'Will do.' And Julie returned to the Hooked on Yarn stall to come up with a plan.

As she pondered, she remembered Neil popping round earlier to say goodbye. 'I'm off to my meeting,' he'd said. 'Followed by drinks.' He rubbed his hands.

'You're very pleased with yourself,' she remarked. 'Considering your usual views on meetings.'

'This is different. Anyway, might see you later, depending how long it goes on.'

'Will the nature reserve trustees be partying late into the night?'

He snorted. 'It's more likely I'll see you than not, but I thought I'd say. Anyway, I'd best not be late.'

Thinking about it now, his manner had been slightly odd. *Is he up to something?*

The line of children round the grotto moved and she glanced at Santa, who met her eyes and immediately looked away. Then he coughed. He spoke to the child opposite him and coughed again.

'I'm just popping over there,' said Julie, for the benefit of her fellow stallholders, and walked to the grotto. She waved at the nearest of the elves, who was gently rubbing her upper arms. Her costume was rather flimsy. 'I wondered if you two and Santa would like a drink. This must be thirsty work.'

'Oh, I'd love a cuppa,' the elf replied. 'Santa, how about you?'

'Yes please,' boomed Santa, still not looking at Julie. 'Two sugars.'

'Can I have a glass of water?' asked the other elf.

'I'll see what I can do,' said Julie, and headed to the kitchen.

Neil would never take two sugars in tea, she

thought, as she found mugs. *Though that could be a double bluff.*

A few minutes later, she took a tray out. 'Hot drinks coming through,' she said to the line, which parted for her. She stopped in front of Santa. 'Here you are.'

'Thank you! Ho ho ho.' He reached for his mug.

He isn't Neil. The fingers aren't long enough, and the tips are square.

Santa took another mug and leaned over to pass it to the chilly elf. *No, this man's too broad to be Neil.*

Julie returned the tray to the kitchen and went back to her stall. She answered Saffron's raised eyebrows with a shrug.

***

Finally, mid afternoon, the demand for soup eased. Saffron had made several attempts to escape from the soup kitchen. However, the furthest she had managed was halfway across the community centre before Roar called her back because someone was asking about celeriac.

'I'm just going to stretch my legs,' she said to Janet. 'You can manage for a couple of minutes, can't you?'

'Oh yes,' said Janet, who was sitting on a camp stool she had brought with her. She nodded at Roar and Chad. 'These two are doing most of the work, anyway.'

'I'll be over there,' said Saffron, waving in the general direction of the grotto. 'Give me a shout if you need me. And don't let the kids serve hot soup. Roar's eleven and generally sensible, but still...'

'Right you are,' said Janet.

Saffron checked her watch. Almost three o'clock: the afternoon was flying by. She wandered from stall to stall, gradually drawing nearer to the grotto. *I bet some megastars have less protection than that Santa.* Then she spied a gap in the line. 'Excuse me,' she said, squeezing through. 'Just, um... Thank you.'

She edged closer.

'Thank you, Santa,' said his latest visitor, a small girl. She got up from her chair and walked off. 'Come on, Mummy.' Santa grinned at the departing pair. His two bottom teeth crossed over a tiny bit.

That's not— He isn't Jamie. He's too slight, as well.

Saffron went back the way she had come, again excusing herself to the line, and stalked to the soup kitchen feeling cross. She saw Julie looking her way and shook her head. *Of course it wasn't Jamie: he's at the football. I know he's at the football. It was silly of me to even think it.*

She seized a ladle and stirred the soup viciously.

6

Of course it isn't Declan, thought Becca. *Ridiculous. He's with his kids – he told me he would be.*

Even so, she had a sneaking suspicion.

It's just . . . that guy I saw earlier, who walked like Declan...

You're being silly now. He's with his kids, you know he is.

The guy had headed for the toilets early in the event. He was well wrapped up in a scarf and a woolly hat. Becca hadn't seen his face, but he was instantly familiar. And she hadn't seen him leave.

From that point, Becca's suspicions had grown. She recalled how vague Declan had been about his weekend plans, and though he had rubbished her idea, still she longed to get a closer look at Santa. The secondhand bookstall and lucky dip were busy the whole time, though, and she only had Ellie to help.

One of the volunteers had said she would come along – several others were running the main bookshop – but she had phoned an hour before the event to say that she had a bad cold and couldn't make it.

In a way, the bookstall had been a victim of its own success. The book lucky dip was so popular that they had almost run out of books twice, and Ellie had had to sneak under the table and wrap some spares. Meanwhile, several people had asked for advice about buying preloved books as Secret Santa presents, and more had arrived bearing carrier bags of books for the shop. Becca wasn't sure whether she would leave with fewer or more books than she had started with.

But at last, it was quiet.

She checked the clock over the door: ten to four! *If I'm ever getting a look at Santa, now's the time.* The line had disappeared and one small boy was left, sitting opposite Santa, with his parents standing behind him.

'Ellie, can you mind the stall for a minute or two? I need the bathroom.'

'Me?' Ellie's eyes were like saucers. 'What if people want to buy things? What if I give them the wrong change? And I don't know how the card reader works.'

'Don't worry about any of that.' Becca put the cash box and the card reader out of sight. 'If anyone comes to buy something, or they have a question you can't answer, tell them your mummy will be back in two minutes to help.'

'Shall I say you're in the loo?'

'No, please don't. Just say I'll be back in two minutes.'

Becca walked in the general direction of the grotto, trying not to seem as if she was making a beeline for Santa.

The boy said 'Thank you,' and stood up. His parents thanked Santa too.

'Any time,' said Santa. 'Ho ho ho!' He leaned over to talk to one of his elves, then caught sight of Becca and beckoned with a long finger.

Becca looked around her. 'Me?'

'Yes,' boomed Santa.

Becca walked slowly towards Santa, feeling her face burn.

'Take a seat,' said Santa.

Becca sat on the chair. It was a child-sized chair and she landed with a bump.

'Have you been good this year?' Santa asked, loud enough for the whole room to hear.

'Um, I hope so.' Someone giggled.

'And what would you like for Christmas?'

Not to be embarrassed by some random man playing Santa.

'Um . . . world peace and . . . for no one to go hungry.' Without waiting for an answer, Becca scurried to her stall, convinced everyone in the room was looking at her.

'I thought you were going to the loo, not visiting Santa,' said Ellie. 'You can still go to the loo if you want. No one's come over.'

'I'll wait,' muttered Becca. Wild horses wouldn't make her go within ten feet of Santa again. But she was sure he wasn't Declan. Firstly, in spite of the obvious tummy, Santa was too tall and thin. His trousers just reached the top of his boots, and skinny wrists protruded from his cuffs. Secondly, Declan wouldn't have put her on the spot.

'Mummy,' said Ellie, 'the scary lady's waving at you.'

'Scary lady?' Becca looked where Ellie was pointing. 'Oh, you mean Saffron. She's not scary. Well, not really. Not usually.' Saffron was mouthing something and pointing at the grotto, but Becca couldn't tell what she meant.

'Mummy...'

'Yes, Ellie?'

'Did you mean what you said to Santa, about wanting world peace for Christmas?' A worried little furrow had appeared between Ellie's eyebrows.

'It would be nice, wouldn't it,' said Becca. 'But a box of chocolates would be lovely too.'

Ellie beamed. 'That's all right then.'

'Back to the North Pole for me!' shouted Santa.

'See you next year!' He strode out of the community centre, flanked by his elves and watched by everyone. And among the spectators were three women who suspected, despite themselves, that something was up.

7

As people wandered outside, stallholders started to retrieve boxes and clear their tables. *That's that*, thought Becca, feeling rather flat.

'Have you had a good day?' said a loud, cheery voice at the door. Becca jumped, thinking Santa had returned, before she realised it was Richard, the vicar. 'Now, why don't you take a break and join in carols round the tree? That would be much more festive, and I'm sure packing up can wait.'

'The room's booked till six,' said Charlotte. 'There's plenty of time.'

'Come along, then,' said Richard. And they had no choice but to follow.

It was nearly dark, and people were heading for the Christmas tree, a black triangle defined by multicoloured lights.

'Look, Mummy,' said Ellie, tugging on Becca's

hand. 'It's beautiful.'

'It is,' said Becca.

Ellie towed her towards the tree, and as they approached, the brass band from the local high school began to play 'Silent Night'.

'Maybe we can get right to the tree!' said Ellie.

'Ellie, stay with me. I don't want you getting lost in the crowd.' Becca hurried after her.

'Look! There's D— I mean Mr Cole!'

'Declan's here?' While Ellie was aware she had to call Declan Mr Cole at school, she occasionally got mixed up.

'Over there!' Ellie waved frantically and took a right turn, weaving through the crowd. Becca followed, with lots of excuse-mes, and presently found herself in front of Declan, his children, and his ex-wife, Roni.

'Wh – I didn't know you were coming.' *What are you doing here* had been on the tip of her tongue, but that felt unnecessarily aggressive.

'Oh, we always come for the carols if we can,' Declan replied. The band segued into 'God Rest Ye Merry Gentlemen'.

'Oh, right,' said Becca. *You didn't mention it last year. Or when I asked about your weekend plans.*

The medley of carols ended with the chorus of 'Oh Come All Ye Faithful'. 'Good afternoon, one and all!'

said Richard, his voice amplified and slightly tinny. 'Welcome to our annual festive singsong! Are you in good voice?'

'Yes,' replied the crowd.

He cupped a hand to his ear. 'You'll need to be louder than that.'

'Yes!' roared the crowd. Becca heard Ellie giggle beside her.

'In that case, let's get cracking. We'll start with "Away In A Manger".'

Becca studied Declan's profile as the brass band played the introduction. He seemed totally absorbed in the music. Her eyebrows drew together, but now it was time to sing.

***

Julie felt a tap on her shoulder halfway through 'While Shepherds Watched'. She turned, and her eyes widened. 'I thought you'd be out with your nature crew.'

'Most of them had the winter sniffles,' said Neil. 'Those who made it. We got through the meeting as best we could and decided to call it a day. So I decided to drive back and help you.' He grimaced. 'I forgot the road closure, so the car's half a mile away.'

A woman shushed him.

'Sorry,' he mouthed. 'When I got to the community centre,' he said, more quietly, 'it was locked, so I figured you'd be in here somewhere.' He put an arm around her waist. 'Fancy a quiet drink when this is finished? I can drop the car off and walk back, or leave it where it is till tomorrow.'

'Why not,' said Julie. 'I'll have to pack up first, but that won't take long.' *Neil never drives if he's having a drink,* she thought. *He always takes a bus or a cab.*

'Oh, I forgot to ask,' he said, when the carol had finished. 'How did it go? I know the topper went off all right, but what about the rest of it?'

'It was good,' said Julie. 'The topper had lots of compliments and we sold almost everything on the stall. And the replacement Santa was quite good,' she added, watching Neil closely.

'That's OK then,' he said. Was she imagining things, or was his tone a little too casual? 'Well done, but I bet you're glad it's over.'

'And now the one you've been waiting for!' the vicar announced. '"The Twelve Days of Christmas."'

I wonder if you're glad it's over too, thought Julie, as the band played the introduction.

***

Saffron, Roar and Chad were singing that they all wanted figgy pudding when she saw a blue and yellow bobble hat approaching through the crowd. As it got nearer, she could also make out a blue and yellow striped football shirt, a scarf, and Jamie.

'Hello there,' he said, and kissed her.

'How was the match?'

Jamie's mouth turned down. 'We lost 3-1.'

'Oh dear.' She couldn't manage to sound very sad. *Serves you right*, she thought, but kept that to herself.

'Did the festival go OK?' asked Jamie.

'Yes, fine,' said Saffron. 'Although I may have over-catered. We've enough soup for the next three months, at least.'

'Did Santa visit?'

'He did, thank you for asking.'

'That's all right then,' said Jamie. 'At least you didn't end up having to do it.' And he winked at her.

Saffron stared, but Jamie had faced the front and was singing away.

Oh well, she thought, and joined in. At least the festival had been a success and Santa had come, even if she didn't know who he was.

8

'Why don't I cook tonight?' said Jamie, when they had finished filling Saffron's freezer with soup. 'You've been on your feet all day, dealing with soup. And people.'

Saffron grinned. 'I've already planned for that. I took bolognese sauce out of the freezer last night: I knew I wouldn't be able to face soup. It just needs pasta to go with it.'

'You still deserve a break. Why don't you have a bath, light candles…'

She raised her eyebrows. 'If you're offering, I won't say no.'

As she poured bubble bath under the running tap, she heard Jamie whistling. *He's in a very good mood, considering his team lost.* She took a thoughtful sip of the glass of red wine she had brought with her. *Hmmm.* She picked up her phone and found Julie's number. *Are you busy?* she texted.

No, in the pub with Neil. What's up?

Nothing really. Saffron mused. *Call me obsessed, but I'm convinced something was going on with Santa. I thought he might have been Jamie, but he wasn't.*

I wondered if he was Neil, but he was too stocky and broad-shouldered.

Saffron frowned. *He wasn't stocky,* she typed. *He had a tummy, but I assumed it was a cushion.*

Well, he definitely wasn't Neil, because Santa's fingers had square tips.

Bubbles rose above the rim of the bath. Hurriedly, Saffron turned off the tap, put her wine and phone within reach, took off her bathrobe and eased herself in. She imagined Jamie downstairs, filling a pan with water... 'Hang on a minute,' she said, frowning.

Jamie's fingers have square tips, she typed. *And he's stockier than Neil, with broad shoulders. But the Santa I saw was fairly slight.*

She sipped her wine, watching the phone for a reply. It came perhaps five minutes later. *Sorry, had to wait a bit as Neil commented on all the texting I was doing. He's at the bar now.*

The phone buzzed again. *So . . . was there more than one Santa?*

'Of course!' cried Saffron, almost pouring her wine into the bath in her excitement. *It's the only explanation*, she typed.

When did you get a look at Santa?

Around three. How about you?

Not long after he came into the community centre. Maybe 2.15. I offered them tea. Santa had two sugars.

Saffron grinned. *The Santa who came off the sleigh was Jamie*, she typed. *He always has two sugars in his tea. He must have done the first part of the Santa shift then gone to the football. So they probably swapped at 2.30ish. The football ground isn't far.*

Julie's message followed quickly. *So the Santa you saw . . . was he Neil? Can you describe him?*

Saffron thought. *To be honest, I just saw he wasn't Jamie. His two bottom teeth crossed over a little.*

In that case, it wasn't Neil. So who was it?

Saffron considered, sipping wine. Now that she had uncovered Jamie's role in what felt like a conspiracy, she was determined to get at the whole truth. Then she remembered Becca scurrying to her stall following her visit to the grotto. That had been minutes before Santa left the community centre. *I'm texting someone else*, she typed. *I have an idea.*

She scrolled to Becca's number. *Weird question for you. Do Declan's two bottom teeth cross slightly?*

That is a weird question, Becca replied. *But yes, they do.*

Can you talk?

We're all watching Arthur Christmas together. I can still text.

Saffron's fingers flew. *OK, I'm putting you and Julie in a WhatsApp group.*

What's going on?

It's a Santa thing. Saffron broke off to give herself a hasty scrub with a flannel.

Saffron: Hello again. *This is what I think happened. The first Santa was Jamie. That's who you saw, Julie. He handed over to the next Santa at about 2.30, and I reckon that was Declan.*

Becca: *That makes sense! I was convinced I spotted Declan going into the toilets quite early on. That must be where they swapped. So that Santa was the one with the teeth?*

Becca: *That sounds terrible, but you know what I mean.*

Julie: *What did your Santa look like, Becca?*

Becca: *I couldn't see much because of the beard and outfit. He was sort of gangly. And he had weirdly long fingers. I saw when he beckoned me over.*

Julie: *That could definitely be Neil. He told me he had a meeting followed by drinks, but he turned up soon after the carols started and said the drinks were cancelled. He took the car, though, which he never does if he's drinking, so he never planned to stay. He must have rushed back, done the Santa swap, then taken off the suit when he left the community centre* *and come to find me.*

Becca: *Declan was already by the Christmas tree with his kids and Roni when I got there. She must have agreed to take them for a bit while he played Santa.*

Julie: *I can't believe it. It's the last thing I'd expect Neil to do.*

Saffron: *I knew Jamie was involved! I just couldn't work out how. He even had the nerve to wink at me when we met at the carols!*

Becca: *I feel a bit bad that Declan went to all that trouble.*

Saffron: *He did it for you. They all did it for us. And the festival, of course. But hopefully, mostly for us.* She considered. *It's rather sweet that they planned it among themselves.*

Becca: *Do we say anything?*

Julie: *I think we should keep it to ourselves. They wanted to keep it secret, so let's do the same. Although there may be an extra present for Neil under the tree.*

Likewise, typed Saffron, and pressed Send. And as she lay back in the bath and finished her wine, she suspected Becca felt the same.

9

Saffron surveyed the committee members on her laptop screen. 'I'll keep this Zoom call brief,' she said, 'as I'm sure we all have lots of Christmas prep to be getting on with. I know I do. So I'll call on you in turn for a quick update.'

One by one, the stallholders reported high footfall, great sales, and positive customer feedback. 'Excellent,' said Saffron. 'So, a generous donation to this year's charities. Paul, anything to report?'

Paul cleared his throat. 'I'm sure you'll be glad to hear that Barry has got over his flu and hopes to be fighting fit for next year.' His eyebrows knitted slightly. 'I had a chat to the elves about the replacement Santa. They said he was very good with the children and played the part well, but they found him a bit... The word they used was changeable. Chatty and friendly sometimes, then they could hardly get two words out of him.'

'I thought he was really good,' said Saffron.

'So did I,' said Julie, with a smile.

'Me too,' said Becca.

'Ah, well,' said Paul. 'Odd how people have different opinions about the same person, isn't it.'

'It is indeed,' said Saffron. 'In any case, another successful Meadley Christmas Festival. I'm liaising with our nominated charities to fix a date very soon to hand over our donations. Hopefully Tim Jameson will cover it for the *Meadborough and District Times*, and you're all invited, of course. And if I don't see you before, I hope you have a wonderful Christmas. Now, let's get off our screens and enjoy ourselves.'

'Hear hear!' the committee responded.

What To Read Next

If you enjoy modern cozy mystery with romance and books, you might like the *Booker & Fitch Mysteries* which I write with Paula Harmon.

As soon as they meet, it's murder!

When Jade Fitch opens a new-age shop in the picturesque market town of Hazeby-on-Wyvern, she's hoping for a fresh start. Meanwhile, Fi Booker is trying to make a living from her floating bookshop as well as deal with her teenage son.

It's just coincidence that they're the only two people on the boat when local antiques dealer Freddy Stott drops dead. Or is it?

The first book in the series, *Murder for Beginners*, is at https://mybook.to/Beginners.

If you love modern cozy mysteries set in rural England, *Pippa Parker Mysteries* is a six-book series set in and around the village of Much Gadding.

In the first book, *Murder at the Playgroup*, Pippa is a reluctant newcomer to the village. When she meets the locals, she's absolutely sure. There's just one problem: she's eight months pregnant.

The village is turned upside down when a pillar of the community is found dead at Gadding Goslings playgroup. No one could have murdered her except the people who were there. Everyone's a suspect, including Pippa…

With a baby due any minute, and hampered by her toddler son, can Pippa unmask the murderer?

Find *Murder at the Playgroup* here: http://mybook.to/playgroup.

And if you like contemporary books with books in them (so to speak), you might enjoy my *Magical Bookshop* series. This series combines mystery, magic, cats and books, and is set in modern London.

When Jemma James takes a job at Burns Books, the second-worst secondhand bookshop in London, she finds her ambition to turn it around thwarted at every step. Raphael, the owner, is more interested in his newspaper than sales. Folio the bookshop cat has it in for Jemma, and the shop itself appears to have a mind of its own. Or is it more than that?

The first in the series, *Every Trick in the Book*, is here: http://mybook.to/bookshop1.

Acknowledgements

My first thanks, as always, are to my brilliant beta readers: Carol Bissett, Ruth Cunliffe, Paula Harmon and Stephen Lenhardt. Thank you for your feedback and suggestions! Any remaining errors are my responsibility.

For *The Book Swap*, I was inspired by the book swap in my home village – it has *two* book swaps, but one is much nearer my house! It's a converted phone box like the one in the story, and I'm a regular visitor and swapper. Thank you to those who maintain it, and to everyone who drops off interesting books there.

I'm lucky enough to live in a place where craft is frequently on display. The bollards in the village centre acquired a Christmassy wrapping, there's a metal 'tree' outside the library decorated with knitting and crochet which changes with the seasons, and I've spotted more than one postbox topper on my walks. At one point I worried that some of my crochet projects in this story were too ambitious – then I checked online and realised that the sky's the limit!

If you're suspicious of Saffron's recipe creations, they can all be found on the web – and I heartily recommend Nigella Lawson's fish-finger bhorta! You can find the recipe here: https://www.nigella.com/recipes/fish-finger-bhorta (we tend to put a bit more veg in to bulk it out). An extra thank you goes to Paula Harmon for coming up with a tinned ham recipe…

And of course, many thanks to you, dear reader! I hope you've enjoyed these stories, and if you have, please consider leaving a short review or a rating on Amazon and/or Goodreads. Reviews and ratings help books find new readers.

COVER CREDITS

Font: Allura by TypeSETit. License: SIL Open Font License v1.10: http://scripts.sil.org/OFL.

Cover image by me (please see copyright page).

About Liz Hedgecock

Liz Hedgecock grew up in London, England, did an English degree, and then took forever to start writing. After several years working in the National Health Service, some short stories crept into the world. A few even won prizes. Then the stories started to grow longer…

Now Liz travels between the nineteenth and twenty-first centuries, murdering people. To be fair, she does usually clean up after herself.

Liz's reimaginings of Sherlock Holmes and her Victorian and contemporary mystery series (two written with Paula Harmon) are available in ebook and paperback.

Liz lives in Cheshire with her husband and two sons, and when she's not writing you can usually find her reading, painting, messing about on social media, or cooing over stuff in museums and art galleries. That's her story, anyway, and she's sticking to it.

Website/blog: http://lizhedgecock.wordpress.com
Facebook: http://www.facebook.com/lizhedgecockwrites
Bluesky: https://lizhedgecock.bsky.social

Instagram: https://www.instagram.com/lizhedgecock/
Goodreads: https://www.goodreads.com/lizhedgecock

Books by Liz Hedgecock

To check out any of my books, please visit my Amazon author page at http://author.to/LizH. If you follow me there, you'll be notified whenever I release a new book.

The Magical Bookshop (6 novels)
An eccentric owner, a hostile cat, and a bookshop with a mind of its own. Can Jemma turn around the second-worst secondhand bookshop in London? And can she learn its secrets?

Pippa Parker Mysteries (6 novels)
Meet Pippa Parker: mum, amateur sleuth, and resident of a quaint English village called Much Gadding. And then the murders begin…

Booker & Fitch Mysteries (6 novels, with Paula Harmon)
Jade Fitch hopes for a fresh start when she opens a new-age shop in a picturesque market town. Meanwhile, Fi Booker runs a floating bookshop as well as dealing with her teenage son. And as soon as they meet, it's murder…

Caster & Fleet Mysteries (6 novels, with Paula Harmon)
There's a new detective duo in Victorian London . . . and they're women! Meet Katherine and Connie, two young women who become partners in crime. Solving it, that is!

Mrs Hudson & Sherlock Holmes (3 novels)
Mrs Hudson is Sherlock Holmes's elderly landlady. Or is she? Find out her real story here.

Maisie Frobisher Mysteries (4 novels)
When Maisie Frobisher, a bored young Victorian socialite, goes travelling in search of adventure, she finds more than she could ever have dreamt of. Mystery, intrigue and a touch of romance.

The Spirit of the Law (3 novellas)
Meet a detective duo – a century apart! A modern-day police constable and a hundred-year-old ghost team up to solve the coldest of cases.

Sherlock & Jack (3 novellas)
Jack has been ducking and diving all her life. But when she meets the great detective Sherlock Holmes they form an unlikely partnership. And Jack discovers that she is more important than she ever realised…

Tales of Meadley (3 novelettes)
A romantic comedy mini-series based in the village of Meadley, with a touch of mystery too.

Halloween Sherlock (3 novelettes)
Short dark tales of Sherlock Holmes and Dr Watson, perfect for a grim winter's night.

For children
A Christmas Carrot (with Zoe Harmon)
Perkins the Halloween Cat (with Lucy Shaw)
Rich Girl, Poor Girl (for 9-12 year olds)

WHITE RHINO BOOKS

Printed in Great Britain
by Amazon